THE SIX
Killer

DILLIE DROAK

This is a work of fiction. The events and characters described herein are imaginary and are not intended to refer to specific places or living persons. The opinions expressed in this manuscript are solely the opinions of the author and do not represent the opinions or thoughts of the publisher. The author has represented and warranted full ownership and/or legal right to publish all the materials in this book.

The Six Killer
All Rights Reserved.
Copyright © 2015 Dillie Droak
v5.0

Cover Photo © 2015 thinkstockphotos.com. All rights reserved - used with permission.

This book may not be reproduced, transmitted, or stored in whole or in part by any means, including graphic, electronic, or mechanical without the express written consent of the publisher except in the case of brief quotations embodied in critical articles and reviews.

Outskirts Press, Inc.
http://www.outskirtspress.com

ISBN: 978-1-4787-0072-2

Outskirts Press and the "OP" logo are trademarks belonging to Outskirts Press, Inc.

PRINTED IN THE UNITED STATES OF AMERICA

Dedication

To my good friend, Clara Garrett (July 10, 1945–December 3, 2014), without her help and encouragement, this book would not have been completed.

Cast of Characters:

Hawk White, Rancher, Deceased
Sue White, Hawk's Daughter
Jim King, Hawk's Heir
Mr. Ryder, Hawk's Lawyer
The Six Killer Ranch, Hawk's Ranch
Brownie, Brazos, and Dingo, Old Hired Hands
Mrs. Irene Murphy, Live-in Housekeeper
Billy, Grady, Mac and Dillard, New Hired Hands
Cookie, Cook for Hired Hands
Mrs. Purdue, Joe Purdue (Chicken Track Joe)
Officer Dirk, Highway Patrol
Mason, Federal Marshal
Tommy Howell, Building Contractor
Don Thomas, Wildcatter
Tom Jacobs, Head of Security Team
Mr. Simmons, Manager of Sale Barn
Black Jack, Dog Trainer
Alex Reynolds, Lawyer

Chapter 1

SUE SAT STUNNED, in deep, glassy-eyed shock, unable to believe what the lawyer, Mr. Ryder, had just read in her father's will.

"It's not true. It can't be true!" she said.

"I'm sorry, Sue. I tried to talk him out of it but his mind was set." Ryder said as he shook his head in regret.

"Why?" she cried.

"I don't know, he wouldn't say why he wanted it done this way."

"So, I'm left with nothing. After all I've done, I am supposed to just walk away from the only home I've ever known, and give my life's work to someone else?" Sue couldn't grasp what he was saying. How could she accept the fact that along with the loss of her dad, she had just lost everything that mattered in her life?

"The new owner requested that you stay on because he doesn't know the ranch," Ryder explained.

"And just who is this new owner? The one my father gave my ranch to?" Sue asked with anger in her voice.

The lawyer swallowed and said, "He's in the next room. His name is Jim King."

"What?" she exclaimed. "He's here?"

"Take it easy, Sue.

"Take it easy?" she said in shrill voice, "Take it easy?"

"Remember, Sue, this is what your father wanted."

"Well, he just slapped me in the face and punched me in the gut. I have no desire at all to see Mr. King. He can go straight to hell for all I care. I will move all my things out of the house now and he can have it."

Ryder cleared his throat and said, "You can't take anything from the ranch. The ranch and everything on it, including the equipment and livestock, belongs to Jim King – all of it."

"The pickup is in my name, that's mine."

"It belongs to the ranch," Ryder explained.

"What?" Sue exclaimed.

"Your father listed it as an asset of the ranch."

"Are you telling me that my pickup is going to the new owner?" Sue asked very quietly.

"I'm sorry, but, yes. It goes with the ranch. Here's a copy of the will." Sue took it, folded it, put it in a rear pocket of her jeans. She didn't want to read it now, in front of anyone else.

"Well, does Mr. King want my clothes, too? Maybe he can wear them or give them to his wife or girlfriend, or am I at least allowed to take them?" Sue inquired.

Ryder was red-faced and irritated by now. Dealing with Sue had been harder than he expected it to be. "Sue, be reasonable, please."

"Be reasonable? Are you insane? After all of the years

I spent working side-by-side with dad. After shoveling out stalls, hauling hay when I couldn't feel my fingers and toes, after all the fence mending, all the herding by horseback, all of that and more, you want me to be reasonable? Well, you can shove it up your – – –!"

"That's enough," another voice said.

Sue spun around and said, "Butt out."

"I can't," said the newcomer.

Mr. Ryder cleared his throat and said, "Sue, meet Mr. Jim King. Jim, meet Sue White." Jim stuck his hand out to shake hers.

She just looked at it and then raised her eyes to his. "Enjoy your new ranch," she said, turned on her heel, and walked out.

The lawyer looked at Jim, shook his head, "It was even worse than I expected."

"What made Hawk write his will this way? I haven't heard from him in years. I haven't managed a ranch in more than ten years. How could he hurt his daughter like this? I don't understand." Jim shook his head.

"I tried to talk him out of it but he wouldn't listen. I can only guess that he didn't think Sue could hold onto the ranch by herself and that a man could manage better. Those are my thoughts. Jim, CAN you manage it?"

He was silent for a few minutes and then he spoke. "I can manage it, but it will take a while for me to get back in the swing of things. How many hands are on the ranch and how many acres?"

"There are three permanent hands and it covers ten thousand acres."

"Whoa! The ranch covers ten thousand acres and there are only three hands?" Jim was surprised.

"Well, with Hawk and Sue, that made five. You see, Sue was a hand, too."

"Sue was a hand, not a daughter?" Jim asked, the surprise showing in his voice.

"Sue was a hand. She was paid as a hand and she did all the housework and cooking. She paid for that pickup out of her wages, but Hawk included it in the ranch assets. He left her nothing but her clothes and I don't know why," Ryder mused.

Sue made it is far as the pickup and opened the door, slid under the wheel and, with her head in her hands, laid it on the steering wheel. She would not cry, not yet. She hurt too badly for that. Why had Hawk done this to her? She thought Hawk loved her. She knew she worked harder than most women her age but she was working for her ranch, or so she had thought. But Hawk had taken that all away from her. Now, what was she going to do? Even the pickup she had paid for wasn't hers anymore. That left her with her clothes and a small bank account. That wouldn't last long. So, where would she go from here? First, she had to get her clothes. Then, find a place to stay and get a job. Most of the local ranches weren't going to hire a woman on as a hired hand and that was all she knew. With the loss of her pickup, she didn't have a way to get to a job if she could find one.

Sue felt so hurt and angry, not able to fully grasp the fact that her father had done this to her. They had worked together as one, rarely arguing, and now, in his final act, her dad had betrayed her. Sue's mind started running out of control, questioning everything she knew and had lived. "Why, why had he turned on her? What could I have done to lead him to this?" Sue quietly whispered to herself as the tears streaked her face.

She jerked her head up when a knock sounded on her door. When she turned, Jim King stood there. He was about forty, and not bad looking, in a rough way. He had broad shoulders, a narrow waist, long legs and lean, hard muscles. His brown hair and hazel eyes set against tanned skin to give King a rugged look. Dressed in traditional western dress pants, shirt and vest, and she assumed cowboy boots, he courteously removed his black Stetson before speaking to Sue. King motioned for her to roll the window down.

"What do you want?"

He looked at her. She had clipped her long auburn hair back off her face. She appeared to be about thirty years old with smooth tanned skin. Sue was about five feet, seven inches and had a pretty good figure, from what he remembered in the lawyer's office, with deep brown eyes that absorbed everything. She wore jeans, boots, a western shirt and a leather vest. A grey hat was on the seat beside her.

"I think we got off to a bad start. I would like to correct that. There are things we need to go over and discuss. There's information that only you know and can give me." Jim informed her.

"That's just too bad, Mr. King. I guess you will have to learn it the hard way like I did. There is nothing I can do to help you. I helped my dad and look what it got me. The clothes on my back plus a few more at the ranch. I'll be packed and out of your way by tomorrow, then it all belongs to you, and you better hope the other hands stay because this one sure won't. I don't know why dad chose you. I have never even heard him mention you, but the lawyer had no problem contacting you. I assume you knew dad from somewhere. Enjoy your ranch and I hope you have to work as hard at it as I did. Goodbye, Mr. King."

She put the truck in gear and drove off. She had selected the blue Ford Ranger with an extended cab when she purchased her pickup. She decided to go to the ranch, pack her things and go for a last ride on Red. Red was a sorrel horse, with a flowing black mane and tail. She absolutely loved that horse. She had raised and trained him from a foal. It was breaking her heart to leave him behind but there was no other choice. Mr. King could get the truck tomorrow. She needed to see about getting some kind of a ride.

Jim stood in the street and watched her drive away. He could understand her bitterness. This was a small town, Rolling Hills, Colorado. Everyone would know the contents of the will before nightfall. It was an awful position for Hawk White to put his daughter in. Hawk had known where Jim was and written to him. He made a request that Jim intended to fulfill, but it depended on him being able to get Sue back on the ranch, and that did not look promising at this time. He got into his black extended cab F250 and started out to the ranch.

Sue had packed the few things she could take from her home, and finished loading them into the truck. She went into the barn, saddled Red, led him out, mounted up, and rode west of the house. The tears wanted to come but she would not let them. Not now. Later, when she was alone, then she would cry. She let Red have his head and he ran over the hills like they were flat. She knew she was going to miss the beauty of her surroundings as she took what she knew would be her last ride. Her eyes blurred with unshed tears, but she trusted Red to get her back to the ranch safely. Her heart was breaking at the thought of leaving the only home she had ever known. With long auburn hair set free, blowing behind her, like the clouds in a breeze, Sue rode fearlessly.

Jim was on the ranch road. He stopped and watched her and the horse. They moved as one. She almost lay on his neck and the horse loved to run. He admired horse and rider. He drove on to the ranch, parked the truck, and climbed out. He was impressed with the location Hawk had chosen for his ranch and head-quarters. There was a small stream that meandered along behind the large barn. There was a cook shack, but there wasn't any smoke coming out of the chimney. Acres of trees stood sentinel behind the barn and on the sides of the small hills around the buildings. The view was fantastic. Hawk had put a lot of thought in his selection of the site before starting construction. As he stood contemplating his friend's will, three men stepped out of the barn. None offered to shake hands. All removed their hats.

"I'm Jim King."

"Sue said you would be along. I'm Brownie." He was at least in his sixties, with gray hair, brown eyes, and stood at six feet tall. He was slim and was dressed in jeans, boots and a western shirt.

"I'm Brazos." He was in his fifties, with slightly graying black hair, and stood about five and a half feet tall. He wore the same kind of clothes as Brownie, but was slightly heavier.

"I'm Dingo." He was in his forties, with longish dark brown hair, offset by light blue eyes. He was slightly heavier, but wore the same type of clothes as Brownie, along with a leather vest.

All three men appeared weather worn and leather tough.

"How come there are only three men? With this much range, there should be more."

"With Hawk and Sue, we had five men. With the range enclosed on three sides, we didn't need more. Now, without Hawk and Sue, you will need more men." Brownie replied as he studied the new owner.

"Did Sue say she was leaving?"

"Oh, yeah, she's leaving. She has no choice."

"What do you mean, she has no choice?"

"With Hawk pulling the ranch out from under her feet, why should she stay? Be a housekeeper for you? Be a cook for us? And have all the gossips in town talking about her being the only woman out here with four men? That would really fix her good, wouldn't it? Hawk took everything from her. Everything! She paid for that pickup with her earnings, but Hawk took that away and gave it to you. When you look at this ranch, you keep in mind that Sue worked side by side with us. Anything and everything that had to be done, she did it. Hawk took it away and gave it to you. She has no reason to stay. Do you think that's fair?" Dingo asked, his anger barely contained.

Jim knew what he said now would determine whether or not he had a crew.

"I don't know why Hawk did it. I don't want the ranch.

I'll give it back to her, some way. It belongs to her. She worked for it and deserves it. I'll even sign the truck back over to her today."

"She won't take it."

"Why won't she?"

"Hawk took it away. He had a pickup, but he took hers and gave it to you. She would do without before she takes anything from the ranch. That house isn't big enough for the two of you."

With that, Jim turned and looked at the house. It was two stories, made of logs fitted together so tight that there wasn't a visible crack anywhere. The bottom four feet were covered in rocks that went all the way around the house, as did the wrap-around porch. As Jim was looking at the house, he heard hoof beats coming rapidly. He turned and saw Sue riding up. Her face was flushed from the ride and the wind. She stopped the horse and dismounted. That's when Jim realized she was riding a stallion.

Without thinking about it, he asked, "What are you doing riding a stallion?" The men were grinning.

"Why can't I? He's just a horse."

"Women don't ride stallions."

"This one does. I raised him from a colt and trained him. He would never hurt me."

With that, she led Red into the barn, unsaddled him, brushed him down and checked his feet. She gave him some hay, checked to make sure the water was working.

She gave him a big, long hug and without a backwards glance, Sue walked out of the barn.

She looked at Jim. "That was my last ride. Now, you'll have to ride him, and take damn good care of him." With that, she got in the truck and drove off, hoping no one caught a glimpse of her tears.

After Sue left, Jim took his things and went in to survey the house. The house was neat and clean. The wood floors were polished to a shine. No dust, no dirty dishes, no dirty clothes. The refrigerator and freezer was both full of food. The pantry was well-stocked. The laundry room was ready for use. Jim would have to ask the men if they ate in the house or the cook shack.

The living room was a large room featuring a massive rock fireplace. The wood box was full, ready to take the chill out of a cool evening. Sheer pale orange curtains covered the two large windows that looked over the yard. A deep brown leather sofa and matching arm chairs provided comfortable seating. Throws were placed casually across the back of each, providing a little color to an otherwise quiet room. A glass topped coffee table held plants and a collection of magazines. Jim could picture Sue and Hawk relaxing here at the end of the day.

The next room Jim entered was the ranch office. Here, a large dark mahogany desk dominated the room. Guests would have sat directly opposite from Hawk in one of the two large sienna colored arm chairs. Antique barrister book shelves lined three walls, filled with books and a lifetime of curiosities gathered on the ranch. A computer and phone sat on the desk, while the printer and fax machine sat on a small stand placed to the left. The file cabinet to the right of the desk held what Jim assumed were ranch records, with a handful of folders perched on a nearby shelf. A large TV hung in the corner of the room and a large colorful rug covered most of the polished wooden floor. Overall the room was well-organized and seemed to be as much of a den as an office.

Jim climbed the stairs leading to the second floor bedrooms. A long, wide hallway ran the length of the second story with a window overlooking the ranch at the far end. A small seating area had been placed there, and Jim could easily picture Hawk relaxing there with a cigar and a glass of bourbon during the long winter evenings.

The first room on the right seemed to be guest room, decorated in blues and gold. Jim closed the door and continued his search. He opened the door straight across from the guest room, which turned out to be Sue's room, featuring the rich browns, reds, and gold he had come to associate with her. She had removed all of her personal belongings already, but the room still carried a hint of her perfume.

The next room to the right was the master bedroom, Hawk's room. It was large, furnished with a solid walnut antique bed and dresser. Like Sue's room, it was mostly decorated in browns, but on the wall hung two spectacular portraits of the ranch. Each captured the same area, but one was painted in the bright colors of summer, while the other was blanketed in snow with twinkling stars accentuating the deep blue of a night's sky. Two floor length windows adorned with sheer lemony curtains provided a breathtaking view. As Jim was gazing at the mountains, he caught his breath at the sight of an eagle slowly circling in the air over the range. The bath and connecting closet were immense. Stacked with towels, wash clothes, hand towels, linens, and robes on this side, and Hawk's clothes on the other, it contained all the luxuries a man could want.

As he left Hawk's room and entered the hallway, he noticed the final guest room to his left. As with the other rooms, the bed had fresh linens and was ready for use. Jim shook his head. How much time did Sue spend in keeping the house so clean? Too much, with all the other things she had to do. He changed clothes and went outside.

"What are you doing tomorrow?" Jim questioned Brownie.

"We will be riding out on the range and checking on the herd."

"Who's foreman?"

"I am, for now," Brownie said.

"What do you mean, for now?"

"I've been here the longest, but thinking about moving on. You know, I started working summers here for Hawk's father and I know this place like the back of my hand, but I don't like the way Hawk shorted Sue. She worked side by side with us. When you look at this place, you keep in mind, that there's as much of her blood and sweat put into it as there is ours. She did everything we did, then she cooked for all of us, did laundry for herself and Hawk, kept house and did most of the paper work for the ranch. All the breeding and calving, she kept all those records. And she got paid hired hand wages. She was more a housekeeper than a daughter to Hawk. For all she did, she got paid less than we did."

"Okay, I see what you mean. Do you eat in the cook shack or the main house?"

"She cooked for all of us."

Jim let out a long breath. "Well, we will have to take pot luck tonight. The fridge is full of food. Can anyone cook breakfast in the morning?"

Dingo said, "I can scare up some breakfast."

"Okay. Do you know any men who want to work? We need a few more hands. I'll be going into town early in the morning. But for now, let's just call it a day."

Chapter 2

SUE FOUND A room at Mrs. Purdue's rooming house. Bless her heart thought Mrs. Purdue but said not a word. She just gave Sue a big hug and showed her the room. It wasn't much, but it was a place to store her things, and she would get two meals a day.

She had stayed in town during the week with Mrs. Purdue while she went to high school. They were old friends, and Sue relaxed as Mrs. Purdue once again told her the story of how she had come to the area.

Mrs. Purdue had arrived as a Swedish orphan girl at the young age of 16. She was too old for the orphanage and was given the choice of domestic service or passage to America as a bride for an unmarried Swedish farmer or rancher who had asked for a wife. Her sister had chosen domestic service and her tales scared Mrs. Purdue so much that she bravely chose the alternative, arriving in America to marry a much older man she had never met.

Her husband had died from a heart attack just a few years after their marriage, but they had been blessed with a son who now lived in Chicago. After the death of her husband, Mrs. Purdue, at that time Mrs. Hanson, bought a large older home and started taking in boarders in order to help pay the bills and raise their son.

She continued to run the boarding house, and eventually married one of her boarders, Joe Purdue, locally known as "Chicken Track Joe". Local legend had it that Joe could track a sage hen or prairie chicken through the brush country.

Joe had disappeared just about the time Sue's father had died. He and Hawk had been close friends and Hawk had used Joe's talents to track down missing livestock numerous times in the past.

Thinking there was something suspicious about Hawk's death Joe had told his wife he would be gone a few days. While this wasn't out of the ordinary, Mrs. Purdue had begun feeling uneasy and had called the sheriff a few days after he left. The sheriff and Sue had alerted the hands, but so far no one had seen any sign of Joe on the ranch.

Feeling overwhelmed with just too much to take in for one day, Sue finally just sat down and cried. After a few minutes, she dried her tears, washed her face and thought, there can be no more tears for me. That's enough. I have too much to do to waste time crying over what's lost. Sue grabbed her keys, climbed in her truck and pulled up at the curb in front of her lawyer's office. With a mix of resolve, dread, and some anger, she locked the truck and went inside.

"What are you doing here, Sue? Why aren't you on the ranch?"

Sue stared at him as if he had suddenly grown two heads.

"What am I doing here? You know darned good and well. I don't have a ranch and I don't have a truck either, so where do you expect me to be? Out on the ranch with three or four men, no other woman there? That is just what all the gossips in town would love. My reputation would be ruined. And, why would I put more of my heart and soul into the ranch now? So here you go, take the keys, the truck is out in front of your office. Enjoy your life, Mr. Ryder, because I sure plan to enjoy mine." She turned and walked out the door.

Jim was up early the next morning and went into town. He needed information and hoped Ryder could help him. He noticed Sue's pickup outside and hurried in.

Ryder handed him the keys and said, "She turned it in yesterday evening."

"What's she driving?"

"I have no idea. She told me some things that I had no idea about. I was sick to my stomach, so I closed the office early and went home. I don't understand any of this."

Jim said he didn't either. He asked Ryder if he knew of a woman who would work as a live-in housekeeper. Ryder didn't, but offered to ask around.

"I want Sue back on the ranch, but I don't know how to get her to come back out there." Jim remarked.

"Why do you want her there, Jim?"

"You know as well as I do that it should have been her ranch. I don't want it and I will definitely give it back to her when I can. I have my own money, I don't need to spend hers. She earned it and it belongs to her."

The uneasy feelings he'd had ever since encountering Sue continued to eat at Jim. He felt awful about the way her dad seemed to have turned on her at the end, and he was unable to fathom what had made Hawk change his will. He knew he had to try to talk her into coming back to the ranch, but didn't have a clue where to start.

It didn't take long for word to spread that Mrs. Murphy seemed like the answer to Jim's prayer. During the interview he learned that as a young girl, the recently divorced Native American woman was taken in by Hawk to care for his wife who at the time was suffering from a long-term illness. Irene's dark brown eyes lit up when she spoke of the time she spent with Sue and her family. After marrying Dan Murphy, she had moved away. She asked him how Sue was doing.

Jim told Irene about Hawk's death and that Sue was currently staying in the boarding house in town, but that he wanted her to come back to the place. He mused to himself that Irene might be just the ticket to getting her back.

Before offering Irene the position, he went back to the ranch and asked the hired men for their opinion. Brownie was the first of the men he encountered. He relayed what he remembered of her past. Apparently Sue had become very fond of her during Irene's time caring for her mother and she was sad when Irene married and moved away, not long after her mother passed away. It was at this point that she and Hawk became inseparable.

Jim had a new insight into just how close they had really been and new sympathy for the girl whose ranch had been taken away from her and given to him. Even if it was for the best of reasons, he could see why she resented him.

He wondered if having Irene would help bring Sue back or drive her further away.

In the meantime there were other things that demanded his attention.

Sue was exhausted after the stress of losing first her father and then the ranch. She sat in her room at Mrs. Purdue's feeling discouraged, and angry at her father, his lawyer, and Jim King.

She went downstairs and tried to eat the supper Grace Purdue had prepared. It was delicious, but having no appetite, Sue had to force herself to eat. Despite the fact that conversation was flowing between the other boarders, Sue quickly excused herself, borrowed the local paper and went back to her room.

About twenty minutes into her search for used trucks and help wanted ads, there was a knock on her door.

Opening it, Sue found Grace Purdue with a plate of warm cookies and a mug of hot chocolate. Sue's thoughts went back to first breakup in high school, when Grace had come to her door to comfort her, bearing the same items.

Sue couldn't suppress a grin, as she invited Grace into the same room that reminded her of that moment. Grace looked at her fondly and said, "I know this is more serious than your crush on that bronc rider, but a few cookies and hot coca can't hurt. You hardly ate two bites of your supper. Do you feel like talking to me dear? You know I am here for you and can keep a secret."

Tears filled Sue's eyes as she replied, "I just can't imagine why Dad did this. Mr. Ryder had no explanation and I want to hate Jim King, but he seems like a kind man, and of course he is pretty good-looking in his own way."

This made Grace smile a bit before she answered, "Sue, I think your dad must have been worried about something. He and Joe had several discussions about something that was bothering him not long before his death. I am pretty certain that is why Joe disappeared. I pray that he is investigating, but am also afraid something has happened to him as well."

"Oh Grace! I hope not, here I have been sitting around thinking about my own problems and forgot about yours. I sure nothing has happened!"

"Well my dear, I'm prepared for anything. I've learned in my lifetime that I can't control everything that happens, all I can control is what I do about it. I will help you in any way I can and I am pretty sure that Hawk did what he did to protect you, although it may not seem like that right now. You know he was so protective of you, especially after Irene ran off with that no good Dan Murphy. He even hand-picked his hired men so that they would be clean, sober, and old enough that you wouldn't be interested in any of them. Oh, and did I tell you that Irene is back in town? She stopped in to see if I needed any help, but I'm not that busy."

Sue brightened at that and replied, "Oh, I'd love to see Irene again, it's sure been a long time. I guess I had better try to get some sleep. I have to find something to drive and a job tomorrow. I'm also going to see what I can find out about Jim King, it looks like I'll have a pretty busy day. I may not be in for dinner, but will try to get back for supper."

Grace picked up the empty mugs and the plate, pausing just before she left the room. "You know I'll help you anyway that I can so keep your chin up, sweetheart."

Relaxed, Sue climbed under the down comforter Grace had thoughtfully provided. Just before dozing off, she reminded herself to be sure and thank her good friend for all she had done for her.

When Jim got back to the ranch, there were new men, waiting for him. They removed their hats as had the other men. The three older hands may not have been happy with the situation but they showed Jim King the respect due him as the owner.

Brownie introduced the men. Billy was the youngest, in his late twenties, with black hair and very dark brown eyes. He stood at six feet tall. In fact, four of the five men stood at least six feet tall. Grady was in his thirties, slim, with brown hair and hazel eyes. Dillard appeared to be in his fifties, with slightly graying thick black hair. Mac was in his forties, sported an impish grin, blazing red hair and eyes as blue as the sky. He stood at just over six feet tall.

All of the men were obviously experienced, without a green horn among them. Each had a saddle horse, equipment, and had worked cattle for years.

Cookie had long since retired from riding horses, and when he walked, he did so with a slight stoop. After years of running a chuck wagon, pounding his bones, on the open prairie, he was looking for a ranch job. In his sixties, Cookie wasn't young anymore, but he was an excellent cook.

"We're all on probation to see if we can work together. Brownie is foreman. You take your orders from Brownie and he takes his orders from me. There is one more thing. Absolutely no one rides the stallion. Do you understand me?" All the men nodded and the three old hands let him know they appreciated what he had done. That horse belonged to Sue, and no one else would ride him.

"Cookie, use the supplies in the house for the next couple meals. Make a list and you and I will go over it, okay?"

Cookie nodded and said, "Yes sir."

"After we finish, do you want to go to town and get the supplies yourself?" Cookie nodded and said that he would get them. Jim told him to put them on his account.

Having decided to hire Irene, Jim added, "One more thing, there will be a lady moving in tomorrow and she will be a live-in housekeeper. Treat her like a lady. If she asks you to do something, do it. Okay?"

The men nodded and Brownie said, "You didn't have to say that."

"I'm glad to hear it, but I have seen men mistreat a woman just because they could. I'm glad you men aren't that way, but I don't know you. We will eventually get used to each other."

Chapter 3

"COOKIE, GET WHAT you need from the pantry and I'll eat with you men tonight. We'll get an early start in the morning. Brownie, I'll ride with you. Brazos, you take two new men. Dingo, you take the other two new men. Cover as much range as you can. We'll double up only a couple of days. After that, we'll all ride single. I may have to hire more men in the long run but we'll give this a try first."

Cookie served an excellent meal. Jim ate, then headed to the house for a shower and bed. Morning would come early.

When he woke the next morning, Jim thought about everything that needed to be done. He knew he faced a big job, including how to get Sue back out at the ranch.

Jim was admiring the view from his windows when he realized he was smelling coffee, and that got him rolling out of bed in a hurry. He was puzzled for a few minutes. As he dressed, he remembered that Mrs. Murphy was to start today. Apparently she started early. He finished dressing and rushed down the stairs and to the kitchen.

Mrs. Murphy was busy cooking breakfast. She told him to sit down. She poured him a cup of coffee, set a plate of bacon, eggs, and potatoes down in front of him.

She sat down with her plate and joined him.

"Mrs. Murphy," Jim began.

She turned and with a smile said, "My name is Irene. Please use it."

Jim grinned and said, "Okay. I didn't expect you so early. I need to show you upstairs and let you pick out a bedroom."

"There's a small room off the kitchen here and that will do fine. I don't need much room. Work on a ranch starts early so I came early. Do you want lunch or just dinner, and what time?"

"I hadn't thought that far ahead. Let's stick with dinner, for now, about seven. I should be in from the pastures by then. Please check the supplies. Cookie will be going into town and can pick up what you need. If you prefer, you go into town and put them on my account."

"Everything looks good so far."

"Then I'll go out to join the men."

Jim checked in with Cookie, and they went over the list.

"See if Irene, the housekeeper, needs you to pick up anything for her."

Cookie smiled and said, "I will check with her and then run into town to pick up the supplies."

After Jim and the hands saddled up, he hollered, "Let's ride, men!"

As Jim and Brownie rode through the pastures, Jim

began to realize what a vast area the ranch covered. There were mountains and hills, arroyos and flats. Everywhere he looked, the view was spectacular. The herd was in good condition, with sleek coats, and baby calves playing alongside the cows. As they rode, they came to a large flat area.

"We use this as a hay field. We get a lot of hay for winter feed from here," Brownie commented.

"It's pretty isolated. Is there a problem with cattle rustling here?"

"Not much. It's hard to steal cattle when there's not a way to access them. We lose some to coyotes, mountain lions, and winter kill, but not many. Hawk used to hire Joe to come out to find strays and check for predators like coyotes and cougars. We'll be driving the herd down close to the home place pretty soon. It makes it easier to feed them and keep track if some are calving in the winter."

Jim was thinking this is the place. He had a feeling that this field would play a big part of whatever was going on. He looked around and liked what he saw. The snowcapped mountains were awesome. He hoped to see the eagle again but didn't really expect to. The sunset was beautiful, reflecting the breathtaking beauty in the clouds that seemed to float on forever. He shook his head and looked at Brownie.

"Brownie, do you ever get tired of this beauty or do you see it any longer? You have been here a long time."

Brownie looked at Jim. "Jim, I see it every day. I will

never get tired of it. Look around you. Things change every day. I love this place."

It was time to return to the ranch. They took the horses into the barn, unsaddled them, brushed their coats, checked their hooves, made sure they had hay and water, and went outside. The other men were just riding in. Good smells were coming from the cook shack. Jim looked at it and decided to build a larger one with a bedroom for Cookie. Cookie rang the triangle and the men went in.

Jim headed to the main house, which beckoned him with the aroma of home cooked food. He hurried up the steps.

"Wash up," Irene told Jim as he entered. "Dinner is ready."

He cleaned up and sat at the table. Irene set a bowl of chicken and dumplings, fresh rolls and butter in front of him. Then, she took her place and they ate. Afterwards, she served hot apple pie with ice cream on top.

"That was some delicious food, Irene."

"Thank you. I love to cook and it makes it worthwhile when someone enjoys it."

"I sure did enjoy it. Did you find everything you need? Do you need things from the store?"

"Everything's already well-stocked. I don't need anything, but if I do, I'll just head on into town and get it. Thank you for asking."

Jim went into the office to take a look at the books and see if anything looked odd to him. He was hoping that Hawk had left him a message or some information about what was worrying him, but Jim found nothing. Hawk had written of some of his concerns in his last letter, but after spending several hours, he was no closer to solving the problem than when he started. Jim was more than just a little frustrated. He was going to have to look elsewhere. The ranch books appeared to be in order. Finally, with a heavy heart, Jim went upstairs to his bedroom.

A good night's sleep and a hearty breakfast put Jim in a better frame of mind the following day. The men were saddling up, ready to ride through the pastures. He asked for a report of conditions and got a good one. The grass was still good, plenty of water. No cattle or calves were down. He saddled his horse and led him from the barn. He had chosen a roan for his horse. He was good looking with a solid build, and was well trained.

"This is the last day for doubling up. Cover as much ground as you can. Brownie, you and I will cover ground that's new to me. See everyone later. Let's ride."

Sue was watching the newspaper for wheels and a job. Both were hard to come by. She knew a little about how to use the computer but not enough for a job. But she did know enough to do some research on Mr. Jim King. Her dad obviously knew him from somewhere in the past. She would see what she could find out. It seemed to her, there was more to this than just the ranch.

Sue had time on her hands so she might as well make use of it. She went to the local library to use a public computer. The first thing she did was sign into her dad's email where she found a cryptic message "To Sue". Without taking time to analyze the entire letter, she took note of the location Hawk told her to check in his office. Next she typed in the name Jim King. She could not believe how many hits she got. It was going to be a chore to find the right one, but she had the time. She couldn't understand why she felt the way she did about him.

Jim didn't know if someone was robbing The Six Killer Ranch or trying to take it over. Hawk's letter left a lot unsaid and Jim couldn't ask just anybody about it. He was new here and didn't know who he could or couldn't trust. He needed to talk to Sue. He didn't know if she would hear him out but he had to try. She needed to be on the ranch. He wanted her on the ranch. He thought to himself, where did that come from? He had not been interested in any woman in a long time, and the feelings surprised him.

Jim had not asked any questions about Hawk's death, but now he was wondering. Was it natural or an accident? Did someone help him along? He needed to look at the death certificate and make his own decisions. He would have to go into town and locate Sue tomorrow.

The next morning, he gave Brownie his orders, had

breakfast, and headed into town. He would see what he could find out about Hawk's death, and see if he could find Sue. As he drove into town, he noticed Sue walking down the sidewalk and decided to follow her. After she entered the library, he parked on the street and went inside. He saw her sitting at one of the computers and walked up behind her. She didn't hear him, giving him the ability to see that she was researching him.

"If you wanted to know about me, all you had to do was ask," Jim said.

Sue was so startled that she jumped up and turned her chair over. She was mad as a wet setting hen.

"How dare you sneak up on me like that?"

"I did NOT sneak up on you. I can't help it if you didn't hear me walking. I followed you in from the street because I need to talk to you,"

"Well, I don't want to talk to you."

"Will you please go back to the ranch? I hired a live-in housekeeper and a separate cook for the bunk house. Irene Murphy is the new housekeeper, she said she remembers you as a young girl. You won't be a hired hand, but you need to be on the ranch."

Sue looked at him but didn't respond to the mention of Irene, making Jim wonder if he had made another mistake. She turned her head and asked, "Why should I go back out there?"

"The ranch is yours. I will find a way to give it back to

you. I don't want it. You worked very hard for it. And Red misses you. I won't let anyone else ride him. He's yours and you need to see him and ride him."

The tears were in her eyes but she wouldn't let them fall.

Jim suggested, "Let's go somewhere for coffee so we can talk. There are things I need to tell you. I'm not your enemy, Sue. I honestly want to help you any way I can."

"Why did Dad give you the ranch?" Sue demanded, wanting answers more than ever to the nagging questions that ran through her mind.

"We need somewhere more private than the library to talk. Let's go get some coffee."

Sue thought about it and then nodded. She closed down the computer and walked out of the door into the blinding sunlight with Jim. They went to her favorite cafe, The Coffee Pot, and found a corner table in the back so they could have some privacy. They both ordered a cup of coffee and a slice of homemade apple pie.

After they were served, Sue looked at Jim and said, "Now what?"

"First thing, how did your dad die?"

Tears immediately sprung into her eyes.

"He was riding alone and his horse spooked for some reason and he was thrown. He hit his head on a rock, and broke his neck."

"Was there an inquest? It sure sounds like there

should have been."

"I don't think so but everything was so fast I don't remember," Sue said softly.

"Was his horse known to spook?"

"No. Normally, he would never spook or throw his rider."

"Was the accident scene thoroughly looked over? Did anyone try to find out what might have spooked his horse?"

Sue blurted, "I don't know. I was so upset I can't remember what all happened about that time." She wiped tears away.

Hawk's death was so recent and Sue's grief was still devastating. She realized that she had never questioned whether it had been an accident.

It was odd that Hawk's normally well-behaved horse had thrown him. Sue was lost in her thoughts, wondering what might have happened. It had all been such a shock at the time that her memories were still a little fuzzy. Now she needed to try to recall all the details surrounding the weeks and months leading up to her dad's accident.

There had been a bad drought and Hawk had ridden out that day to check whether there was enough grass and water in that pasture for the herd to stay a few more days.

When he hadn't returned by evening, they went to look for him. There had been a bad thunderstorm and she remembered thinking that at least the drought was over.

Dad will be pleased about that.

Then they rode up on him, a sight she would always remember. His head bloody from where he had hit his head on the rock, the water from the rain pooling around his worn leather boots, his horse patiently standing waiting for him, his saddle soaked from the rain.

Sue's distant eyes brimmed once more with unshed tears, her overwhelming grief threatening to spill down her cheeks.

"Okay." Jim paused before gently continuing his line of questioning. "Are you losing cattle? More than is normal? Is anything strange going on around the place, things that seem just a little odd? Are there trails that shouldn't be there? Is there anything?"

Sue thought a long time. Jim drank some coffee, and ate some pie. He wasn't going to rush her. Let her think things over. She had to wrap her mind around things to see them. He finished his pie, pushed the plate aside, and waited. Sue drank some coffee and set her pie aside as she thought about the questions he had asked.

"There were some things that seemed a little off but I can't remember now just what they were. I'll remember them in time. As for the cattle, I don't think we have lost any. We'll be driving them down to the home pasture pretty soon and then we can get a count on them. The only other thing that comes to mind is that there were lights one night where there shouldn't have been lights. I thought it was odd at the time."

Jim questioned her, "Do you know where they were?"

"No, just a reflection I saw on the skyline," Sue said trying to remember more. "The lights were behind some hills. Why are you asking all these questions?"

Jim finally let her have it with both barrels and said, "Your dad sent me a letter and said he was having some problems and he wanted me to help him figure out what was going on. He died before I could get here to help him. You can't tell anyone what we talk about, Sue. It could mean your life or mine, maybe both. I think someone is trying to take The Six Killer Ranch away from you. Your dad gave it to me to try to protect you. He feared for his life and yours. Do you understand what I'm saying?"

Sue swallowed and nodded her head.

"That's why I really want you back on the ranch, so that I can try to protect you. If none of the men are involved in this, then the old hands will protect you with their lives. They all think the world of you, and you should see how Irene's eyes sparkle when she talks about you. I want you to come back to the ranch. Will you?"

Sue drank the last of her coffee, pushed her cup aside, "What will I do out there?"

Jim said, "You can keep the books and records like you've been doing. You can start a garden if you want. I'm going to build a larger cook house and put a bedroom on the back so Cookie can sleep there. Irene is now officially the live-in housekeeper. She wants to be addressed as "Irene" and she is a good cook as you already know. Your pickup will be your ride. As soon as I can straighten things out, everything will be put in your name. Like I said before, I don't want your ranch. I have money of my own so I'm not using Six Killer money."

Sue responded, "If you're making improvements to the ranch, use ranch money. You have the authority to do for that."

"Are you sure you want me to spend it on that?"

Sue, thinking of the men, said, "Yes, for the cook house and the men's wages."

"Okay. I'll pay Irene out of my money as I'm the one who hired her. But, I think you'll enjoy getting reacquainted with her. So, will you come back to the ranch? And don't tell anyone what we talked about. Not even Ryder. At this point, we can only trust ourselves. At least, I hope you trust me. I trust you to keep this information to yourself." Sue quietly nodded her agreement, lost again in her thoughts.

Chapter 4

SUE AND JIM went to Mrs. Purdue's boarding house and packed up Sue's belongings. They headed back to the ranch. When they got there, the men were in for the day and the old hands came running to hug Sue and welcome her home. They let Jim know they approved. Jim introduced her to the new men and Cookie. She went into the barn to say hello to Red. They heard him welcoming her and all the men smiled. She patted his neck, gave him a big hug and quietly talked to him. When she finished, they went into the house. Irene was in the kitchen and Jim introduced the two, just before Irene gave her a big hug.

"Welcome home, Sue. We are just thrilled to have you back. Dinner will be ready in twenty minutes or so."

Jim took Sue's things to her room and set them down.

"Welcome home, Sue. I'm so glad you're back out here, I've missed you so much."

The tears filled her eyes.

"I didn't think I would ever come back. I'm glad to be here, too."

Jim left her to put her things away and get settled back in. When she came down, he gave her the truck keys.

"These belong to you. All I ask is that you let me

know when you go out. Not that I'm checking on you, but keep in mind what we talked about. I want to keep you safe. We need a code for trouble if it comes to you. What do you suggest?"

"Do you think it's that bad?" Sue was beginning to get worried.

"I don't know yet, but I don't want to take that chance," Jim replied. "What do you suggest we use?"

Sue paused and said, "Let me think on it a while. I'll tell you after dinner."

"Okay," Jim agreed. "There is one more thing and this may be harder. I don't want you to ride Red by yourself. I know you like to ride alone but you could be taken by someone or they may try to hurt you. Can you not ride alone?"

"You're scaring me. Am I in that much danger?"

"I don't know but until I find out what's going on, I'd rather be safe than sorry. You can make an excuse to ride with one of the men but not the same one every time or I could ride with you. I still haven't seen all of the ranch and you could be my tour guide."

"I can do that," Sue responded evenly.

"I haven't seen the place where Hawk had his accident. Can you show me where that is?"

"Yes, I can show you and I won't ride alone." Sue replied after thinking it over.

"It may look like we're involved if we ride together too

often, can you handle that? That's why I want you to ride with the other men. We don't want tales getting started that would ruin your reputation." She blushed but agreed to Jim's plan.

Jim remarked, "I'll be out on the range a lot of the time. I will be looking things over and trying to find out what is so important on this place that someone would want to kill for it. Have there been any oil samples taken from any place on the property?"

Sue hesitated and said, "Not that I know of. There aren't that many places where drilling could be located. Not unless they want to level some land. We are surrounded by mountains."

"Maybe you could show me where the light reflected that time. How long ago was it?"

Sue thought for a few minutes and said, "I think I can locate the place with the lights now, but I can't remember when it was. But it will come to me. Something will trigger my memory and then I can figure out when."

"Okay."

About that time, Irene called them to dinner. The food Irene served was delicious. There were fried chicken, mashed potatoes and gravy, green beans and peach cobbler for dessert. All three ate their fill.

Jim said, "Irene, I won't be able to get into my clothes if you kept feeding me like this."

Irene just laughed. "When you work on a ranch, you

need good food and plenty of it."

Sue helped clear the table but that was all Irene would let her do. Sue and Jim went into the office.

Sue began, "What do you think of "Red" as a "no help needed" code word? If I say the words "Red stallion," then you know I need help. If I just say the word "Red," that means I can handle it by myself. I've worked hard all my life. I think I can handle one man by himself. But if it's two, or maybe a rope, then I'll need help."

"Okay, "Red" it is. I'm going out to talk to the men for a while. I need to get a report from today's ride."

Jim stepped outside and walked over to where the men were. He stepped into the cook shack.

"Cookie, do you have everything you need?"

Cookie grinned and said, "Yes sir, for now."

"I'm going to build a larger cook shack for you. Do you have any suggestions?"

Cookie smiled and said, "Yes Sir. I will need a larger fridge and freezer so I can keep more meat and fresh items than I can now."

"What about adding a bedroom in back?"

Cookie grinned and said, "That would be fine."

"We should get started on it in the next day or two." Cookie nodded.

Jim went out to talk to the men. The report was the same as the day before. He told the men, "We need one more cutting of hay from that field that Brownie and I checked out."

The men groaned, but there were no complaints. It was part of the job. With everyone helping, the hay cutting wouldn't be too bad on any of them. They would cut it in one day, wait one day and haul it the next. After that, he wanted the men to start moving the herd in closer. Winter would soon be on them. They could start moving the herd the day after hauling the hay.

Sue was working on the paper work in the office when Jim came in. She had already found the letter from Hawk personally addressed to her. Having recovered from her surprise and shock of reading about the stress he was under and how well he had hidden it, she was thrilled to find that he had trusted her implicitly while trying to protect her. He had enclosed a recent update to his will, newer than the one they were operating under, leaving her the entire ranch and other property in the event Jim turned out to not be the man Hawk thought he was. She had decided to keep quiet about what she had found, as Hawk had implored in his letter.

"Sue, let me know if something seems even a little off in the paperwork. We have to get a handle on what's going on around here."

"I will do my best, surely I would notice anything that was off."

Jim went upstairs, showered and went to bed. He had to be up early. The haying would give him a chance to thoroughly look over the area without tipping his hand.

Sue went to her room, showered and went to bed. She lay awake for a while thinking things over. She realized she had misjudged Jim badly. She wondered why her father hadn't said anything to her about any problems. She realized then that he had loved her, but was not one to show it. He did what he thought was best for her in the long run and tried to protect her. Alone, she would never be able to find out what was wrong. Hawk trusted Jim to do it. Jim must be some kind of detective -- maybe that's how he earned his money by solving other people's problems. She hoped he could solve hers but she would still keep her eyes and ears open for information to help him. She finally drifted off to sleep now that she had made peace with her father.

Jim was an early riser, but so was Sue. They met in the kitchen where Irene had their breakfast ready.

"Sue, we're going to mow hay today. Would you be willing to drive the tractor in a couple of days so the men could load the bales?"

"No problem," she said.

Jim left with the men, heading to the hay field. They had it all cut by quitting time. With eight men mowing, it didn't take long. When they got back to the house, Cookie had a big spread ready to feed the hungry crew.

"I'll see you in the morning," Jim said as he headed to the house.

Jim went into the house where Irene had dinner almost finished.

"I'll be back down in a minute. I've got itchy hay all over me. I've got to shower before supper." Jim remarked as he headed upstairs.

Irene and Sue laughed. Jim showered, put on fresh clothes and was back in the kitchen, ready to eat, in less than twenty minutes. Irene served roast beef, gravy, green beans and chocolate cake.

Jim moaned. He had eaten too much again.

He looked at Sue. "Have you decided if you want a garden or not?"

"I want one but I think it is too late in the year to start one now."

"Well, go ahead and make your plans now for the garden and any flower beds you want to put in. We can buy a tiller so you will be able to do the work yourself."

"When do you want your day off?" Jim asked Irene.

Irene responded, "I would like half days and I want to take one tomorrow afternoon and visit some friends. I'll leave supper in the fridge and perhaps Sue can warm it up. I'll be back by eight o'clock."

"No problem, I'll warm it up."

"Sue, could you ride out with me tomorrow? The men are starting to push the herd close to home. Maybe we could check out a couple of places."

Sue understood what he was saying and replied, "I would love to give Red a ride. I've missed him. I'll show you some of the ranch, too."

"We'll ride out after the men have left." Sue agreed. Everyone was up early the next morning. The men were saddled up and ready to ride when Jim and Sue went out. Sue slipped into the barn to saddle Red. He was happy to see her.

"Everyone, keep an eye out for each other. We don't want anyone hurt. And, as you know, when pushing cattle, anything can happen. Sue is going to take Red out and show me some more of the ranch. If any of you have trouble, fire your gun three times and we'll come help you."

The three old hands were happy to hear that Sue was going to be riding Red again. They looked at Jim and nodded their heads, before riding off.

Jim saddled his horse and Sue brought Red out of the stable, saddled and ready to go. It was a pleasure to watch the two of them, they loved each other and it showed. That horse would not hurt her in any way. They headed out, riding side by side.

After a little while, they gave the horses their head and let them cut loose. Jim thought that stallion is some horse. With the right mares, he would sire excellent foals. He would have to talk to Sue about it. They pulled the horses in and slowed them down, cooling them off.

"Sue, Red is a fine stallion. Have you considered using him for stud and raising some colts? With the right mares, you could make some money. It would be a slow income but a good one. You'd probably make more if you trained the colts before you sold them."

Sue was quiet for a long time. "I have never considered it, but it does interest me. Where would we get the mares?"

"We could go to some auctions and look around, see what we can find. It isn't something that has to be decided today. Just think about it, okay? Red is a beautiful animal."

Sue considered what Jim had said. "I'll give it some thought. I'm used to working and this sitting around is getting to me. I'm not complaining, I just need something to do."

"That's why I suggested a garden and flower beds. There's a lot of work once you get them going. It will be everyday work. You will have to till, row, plant, fertilize, weed, harvest, may even have to can or freeze things, if they grow well. Flowers always need to be weeded and dead-headed."

Sue looked at him in surprise.

"You seem to know a lot about that kind of stuff."

He looked pained for a few minutes and then said, "I was married once. My wife passed away. She loved her garden and her flowers. She spent a lot of time there. That's how I knew you could fill your time. Give you something with purpose. We can always use fresh vegetables and flowers are always nice in a house. With Red, you could have something else to do. How far are we from the site of Hawk's accident?"

"Not too much farther. We have been going over ground you haven't covered, haven't we?"

"Yes, I haven't been this way before. You have good range. Quality grass, good water, and enough cover for protection. It's a good, balanced ranch, but I don't see anything outstanding. So, whatever is worth killing a man for has to be under the ground. We need to see if someone has had an oil sample analyzed. You may have oil under here somewhere, and people have been known to kill for that kind of wealth. Do you know if anyone ever made Hawk an offer for the property?"

Sue thought about it. "No, but I'll go over the papers in the office. If someone made an offer, Dad did not throw it away. He kept everything. It's there somewhere. We always filed things away in a folder or copied them onto the computer. He may have done that so I wouldn't see it. That makes the most sense. There, that's where he fell, by those boulders."

They rode over there and dismounted. Jim started looking around. He circled out farther and farther with each circle. It had been a while since the accident and he didn't really expect to find anything. But, he kept looking, increasing the circle each time. Finally, Jim spotted something that seemed odd, but it made no sense to him. He called Sue over and showed it to her.

She stood looking at it for a long time. Then she said, "It reminds me of something but I can't place it now. It'll come to me in a little while. It's connected to something else that's hazy in my mind. I need to do some paper work and let it simmer. That's when I do my best thinking."

"You know there was so much rain the day of the accident that any tracks or clues would have been washed away. I'm just afraid we may never find out what happened to Dad."

"That's okay. Darn Sue, I wish I had thought to bring a camera."

"My cell phone has one on it." She took several pictures from different angles. "I'll download them on the computer and make a disk, just in case something happens to the computer. Then, I can make prints."

"Okay. Let's ride by the hay field. I want to check the hay and see if we can haul it tomorrow." They mounted and rode away. They didn't notice the man who rose from behind a small hill a distance away. He couldn't hear what Jim and Sue said, but saw that they had taken pictures of something. He went over the small hill to his vehicle, waited a few more minutes before he started up the engine, wanting to make sure they didn't hear him. Then he drove away.

Chapter 5

WHEN SUE AND Jim rode back to the ranch, they met up with the rest of the crew. After the horses were unsaddled, Jim told the men they would be hauling hay the next day. Sue would drive the tractor while the men loaded the hay. The men headed over to the cook shack and Jim and Sue went to the house. A few minutes after they had finished eating, there was a knock on the door. Jim went to answer it.

Brownie said, "I need to talk with you, Jim." Jim invited him in. "No. Thanks, Jim. Let's take a ride."

Jim agreed. They got into the pickup and drove down the road about a mile.

"This is far enough." Brownie commented.

He looked at Jim for a long time, said, "Today I was out riding in the pasture close to where you and Sue were. I wasn't watching you, just checking things. I saw you by the boulders where Hawk had his accident. After you rode away, I waited a little while. I saw a man come from behind a small hill, he stood and watched you and Sue for a few minutes then went over another small hill. I waited to see what happened next. In a few minutes, I heard a vehicle start up. I waited a little while, and headed that way. There were several tracks in that area. It wasn't the first time he had been there. What is going on, Jim?"

Jim looked at Brownie and said, "I don't know you very well but I think you're loyal to Sue. Here's what I know." Jim told Brownie everything he and Sue had discussed. "See what I'm up against? Have you noticed anything odd around the ranch? Do you think there is something that's not quite right? Do you know if an oil sample has been taken? Is there anything you want to tell me?"

Brownie was silent a few minutes, "No, I don't know about any oil sample that's been taken. Things seem okay. I haven't noticed anything odd. But I'll be on guard and start paying more attention. Did you find anything around the boulders?"

"Yes, we found some odd marks on the ground. Sue seems to think that she'll remember where she's seen them before. I hope so. Where can I find out if an oil sample has been taken? Where would Hawk's inquest report be?"

"That would be the County Courthouse in Benton, about thirty miles east. If there even is a report, you know things were pretty hectic when Hawk died. Oil sample report would be in Denver."

Jim sighed and said, "Okay. Keep this to yourself for now. If things get rough, I'll talk to the men."

"Okay."

"Let's go, then." Jim started the truck and drove back to the ranch house.

When Jim got back, he invited Sue into the office.

He told her what Brownie had seen and that he had told Brownie everything.

"I need to call someone to build the new cook shack. Who should I call?"

"Tommy Howell," Sue responded. "He runs a family business and it's been around here a long time."

"Okay. I'll call and set up an appointment." Jim made the call and made arrangements to be there at nine o'clock the next morning.

"I know what spooked dad's horse."

"What? When did you figure it out?" Jim blurted.

Sue said, "I thought about it when I was doing paper work. That's how it works sometimes. I just let it alone and up it pops."

Jim said anxiously, "What was it?"

"It was a flag trip."

"How does it work?"

Sue explained, "The flag lies down on the ground and when the trigger is tripped, the flag pops up. It would make any horse spook. The same principal is used in calf roping at the rodeo. Those men must have waited and watched for him for days. They also had to lure him in so that the horse would trip that trigger. Otherwise, dad's horse would not have spooked. They may have killed him. He may not have broken his neck when he fell, they had to do it."

"Grace said she is worried about Joe, he was suspicious

and went out to scout around right after we found Hawk. He still hasn't returned and we're afraid they might have killed him too." Sue's voice cracked and she nearly broke down, unshed tears filling her eyes.

Jim pulled her into his arms and held her as she softly cried.

"Sue, are you okay now?"

"I'll be okay, it just hurts so much." Her father's loss now seemed even more tragic, once she realized it may not have been an accident, but that he may have been killed.

"Let's quit for tonight."

The next morning, Jim met with Tommy. They agreed on what Jim wanted for the cook shack. Tommy would order the fridge and freezer and have his crew there the next morning. The men hooked the wagon up to the tractor, and Sue headed to the hay field. It took several trips to move all of the hay, and they were late getting in to eat. Cookie had supper ready but waited until the men had showered and cleaned up before ringing the triangle.

"Sue, do you have an aerial map of the ranch?"

"Yes, I do," Sue went to the office to find it, and Jim followed.

Sue started searching through Hawk's computer while Jim was looking at the map. A few minutes later Sue gasped.

"What's wrong?"

She pointed at the computer.

Jim went behind her to see the screen. There, he saw an email message that read, "You may as well just give up. You can't keep that ranch. We will take it, one way or another."

"What does this letter mean, Jim? Was someone trying to take the ranch away from dad?"

"That's what I'm trying to find out. Have you had any offers for the ranch?"

"Not that I am aware of, but obviously Dad didn't share everything. We have a lot of paperwork and emails to go through, but I haven't really had enough extra time to check them all out."

"Okay Sue, listen to me. We are going to take this very seriously. First thing tomorrow, I'm going to the court house to see what I can find out about an inquest and anything else that might be related to Hawk's death. I'll get pistols for you and Irene while I'm in town. Do you have any guns here in the house?"

"Yes, we have a rifle and a shotgun. I have my pistol, holster and belt that I always wear when I am out checking pastures."

"Put the rifle and shotgun in a place where you can get to them in a hurry. Let's talk to Irene."

They told Irene most of what was happening.

"Irene, this could be dangerous, do you want to leave?"

She immediately said, "No, I will stay right here, but

leave that shotgun with me."

"Okay, but I am also going to pick up a pocket pistol for you. No man would look in an apron pocket for a gun," Jim said as he grinned at her.

"Jim, pick me up one too!" added Sue.

Chapter 6

THEY ROSE EARLY the next morning. Jim went out to talk to the men. He was filled with dread, worried that there would be more trouble ahead, and what it could mean for the future of everyone involved, unable to shake the feeling that more trouble lay ahead.

"Men, things could get a little rough around here for a while. If any of you want to leave, there will be no hard feelings." No one moved.

"Okay. Each of you strap on a gun. If you don't have one, I'll get you one. Ride in pairs, watching each other's backs. Cookie, what are you going to do?"

"I'll just strap my gun on," Cookie answered with a smile.

"Okay. Brownie will stand guard today. Stay in the barn and stay out of sight. There is to be absolutely no smoking. I don't know what to expect. You men ride careful and pay attention. Be safe. Start pushing the herd down here toward the home pasture. It may be a little early, but it will keep you from being targets out on the open range. Keep your eyes open. Cookie, you keep your eyes open, too. You and Brownie have to remain alert and on the lookout."

Jim went into the house and told Sue and Irene there

was a guard in the barn. He was headed to the courthouse and would get their pistols. He drove to Benton, got his information and headed back to town. He stopped, got the two pistols and headed back to the ranch. He could look the information over closer in private.

Jim gave the pistols to Irene and Sue. Irene checked her gun. She loaded it up, put the safety on, and put it in her apron pocket. She then proceeded to finish cooking dinner. Sue checked her gun, loaded it, and put it into a vest pocket. Jim shook his head. He did not want to be the one who messed with those two women. Jim went into the barn and called Brownie. He did not see him but when he turned around, there was Brownie.

"The women have their guns. Think we could go out to those tracks?"

"Yes sir." Brownie chuckled at the news that the women had guns.

"Let's saddle up. I hope nobody is dumb enough to mess with those two armed women," Jim muttered, more to himself than Brownie. They rode out to where the tracks were. They looked them over thoroughly, but didn't find anything that would identify them.

"Let's follow them and see where they go." They followed the tracks for about an hour.

"I think they are headed for the old county road." Brownie told Jim the road was in bad shape and was used mostly by deer hunters in the fall. The county would grade it about once a year.

"Can we get to it another way?"

"Yes sir."

"Let's go by the hay field."

"Why go there?" Brownie was puzzled.

"I want to see if anything strikes me as odd."

Brownie nodded his assent and they rode to the hay field. He looked at Jim, but said nothing.

"Now we will ride around slowly and take a hard look at the ground."

"What are we looking for?"

"Oh, a hole where the oil sample was taken. I think it will be around the edge of the field. It will be a five-inch circle." Jim felt sure there had been a sample taken.

They started riding around the hay field with about five feet between them. They were about half way around when Brownie motioned Jim to come closer. There was a five-inch circle.

"Is this what we're looking for?"

"Yep, that's it. Let's go."

They rode back to the ranch. The other men were coming in and taking care of their horses.

Jim asked worriedly, "Any trouble?"

"No Sir".

Just then the dinner bell rang, "All right, that's it for today, boys. I think we need a guard tonight. You men work out how you want to do it. Brownie, you and I are going for a ride tomorrow." Brownie nodded.

During supper, Jim told Sue about the hole in the hay field.

"It's a shame some people are so money hungry they will do anything to get it. Jim, what are we going to do now? Do you think this is what Dad was worried about?"

"I'm not a hundred percent sure yet, but Brownie and I are going to drive that county road and see if we can find any clues. I think that you and I should go to Denver to the oil company and see what we can find out. Right now though, I am worn out, let's call it a night and talk in the morning."

The next morning, Jim reminded the men to be extra careful while they were bringing the herd in. He did not want them taking any chances.

Jim and Brownie got into the truck and headed out on their mission. The old county road was as rough as Brownie had warned, and then some. Jim didn't think it had been graded in over a year. After a while Brownie said they were pretty close, cross country, to where the tracks were. Jim slowed down so they could try to see any tracks on the road, but it was almost impossible because the road was rough as a washboard.

They continued driving for a short time then stopped to get out and look at the road again. As they opened their doors, shots were fired at them. They both hit the dirt instantly, but that didn't do any good. The shots kept coming. They climbed back into the truck. Jim put it in gear and drove toward the shooter who lost his nerve and took off on an ATV.

Brownie muttered, "Well, we can't follow that one."

"Where does this road go?"

"I don't know. I haven't been on it in a few years. It was an old logging road and just kind of divides off into a number of trails and finally disappears when you get further up into the timber. Deer hunters still use it to haul their game out, but that's about it." Brownie replied as he looked around them.

"Well, let's just see where it goes then."

Brownie paused then said, "You know, there used to be a few mines up there, but they never amounted to much. It was rumored that a gang of rustlers were up here in the early days, some pretty mean hombres and that's how the ranch got its name, The Six-Killer Ranch." As I recollect the gang got in a shoot-out with the posse and killed several of them. That was way back when Jawk was a little boy. Most of this heavy timber is on public land and isn't much good for grazing. Since the copper and silver that was rumored to be here didn't amount to much, the road was pretty much abandoned. Chicken Track Joe used to go up there after predators when we were losing a lot of livestock, and deer hunters use it once in a while, but otherwise no one travels it."

They started out again and hadn't gone far when they

came to a roadblock. Brownie got out of the truck and was looking around. He called Jim over and showed him the foot prints.

They climbed into the truck and Jim backed down the road until he found a place to turn around.

"Brownie, do you think I could get the county to remove that road block?"

"I don't know, but the deer hunters will sure raise all kinds of hell if they can't get through to go hunting. You might as well call."

"I'll call and see what happens. Sue and I are going to Denver tomorrow to see the oil company. Maybe we can find out something there."

They drove back to the ranch and Jim gave Brownie his orders for the next day before going into the house for the night. After dinner, Jim went upstairs, took a shower and went to bed. Sue wasn't far behind.

Irene had a large breakfast ready for them when they came down the next morning. Jim and Sue left, headed for Denver after checking on the progress of the new cook shack. They were about halfway there, when Jim asked Sue if she would like to stop. She said yes, she needed to stretch her legs and move around some.

"Would you like something to eat? I could sure use some coffee, and maybe a piece of homemade pie."

Sue laughed at Jim. He was hungry all the time. "That sounds good to me." They found a table, sat, and ordered.

After they had eaten, they got into the truck and started driving again. They had pulled into a truck stop, and the big rigs were beginning to roll again. Since they weren't in a hurry, they let the trucks pass and go on. They were behind one, a red K.W., pulling a flatbed trailer loaded with flat sheets of steel, when another one pulled out to pass. The passing truck was a black Pete pulling a flatbed trailer loaded with stacks of lumber.

Suddenly they were hit from behind so hard it was all Jim could do to keep from going under the trailer. Before he could get straightened out, they were hit again. It was all he could do not to lose control. They were hit hard a third time. By now, the truckers realized something was wrong. The black Pete that had pulled out to pass them, dropped back and slid in behind Jim. It protected the rear end of the truck. Another one, a blue K.W. pulling a reefer trailer, pulled up beside him. They were surrounded by big rigs and the other truck couldn't get to them to hit them again. The big rigs began slowing down and when slow enough, started edging to the shoulder. When they stopped, one driver jumped out of his truck, asked if they were hurt, needed the EMTs or anything. Jim looked at Sue.

"I think I'm okay, just startled," she replied.

Jim got out and talked to the driver. "We're okay. Just shook up some. Thank you for your help. I don't know if I could have kept from going under that trailer or going over the shoulder. Thank you again, and please, relay my thanks to the other drivers. You probably saved our lives." Jim was almost in tears, the episode bringing back his own painful memories. They had come so close to being killed.

The trucker said, "I've called the Highway Patrol. An officer should be here shortly. You sure you're okay?" Jim nodded. Then, a siren sounded. The car pulled up and an officer got out.

"You two okay?" the officer asked.

When they both replied in the affirmative, the officer said he had to get the trucker's report and would be back.

"I'm Officer Dirk. What are your names?" Jim introduced himself and Sue.

"I have the trucker's statement about what he saw. Can you tell me what happened?" Jim told about being hit and having a hard time holding his truck in the road.

"Can you tell me what might have brought on this kind of attack?" Jim looked at Sue and she nodded. Jim told the officer the whole story.

Officer Dirk shook his head. "You could have been killed if you had been pushed under that trailer."

"I know. I don't know if I could have held the truck through another hit. I believe those truckers saved our lives."

Officer Dirk agreed and asked where they were headed.

"Denver. I'll have to find a loaner until I can get this one fixed."

"Let's take a look and see how bad it is." They went around to the back of the truck.

"I don't smell any gas and don't see any on the ground. I think it will be safe to drive it to Denver. The small dealers around here won't have a loaner. Here, call this number and he will give you directions and he'll have something ready to go when you get there. Also, I think you should see the Federal Marshal."

Jim looked at Sue. "We plan on doing that."

"Here is his number. Call him and he will give you directions to his office. I won't put this in my report. The reports are public, and you need some time to find out what's going on. You two be careful and have a safe trip the rest of the way to Denver."

"Thank you for your help and you be careful." He gave them a little salute tap on his hat.

Sue looked at Jim, "How are you? Are you feeling alright?"

"Yeah, I'm fine. All of these nice people make up for the bad ones. Are you ready to go?" She nodded.

When they got twenty miles out of Denver, Sue called the dealer for directions. He looked at the damage and said it would take at least a week to order the parts and do the repairs.

He walked them over to another truck and said, "This is my loaner. Use it until I get yours repaired." Jim and Sue thanked him and asked directions to the oil company.

When they located the building, they went in and talked to the gentleman seated at the desk. He asked for Sue's ID, and said that yes, Hawk White had ordered an oil sample to be analyzed. They asked for a description but it wasn't much help.

Next on their list was a call to the Federal Marshal. He gave them directions and was waiting when they arrived. Jim and Sue introduced themselves and he said he was Marshal Mason. He was six feet tall, slim but muscled, had black hair and hazel eyes. He appeared to be very capable and able to handle himself in any situation. Jim and Sue liked him at once. Officer Dirk had called and explained what had happened earlier, but he wanted the whole story from them. They explained the story from the time of Hawk's death, elaborating every detail.

"You sure need some help and I'll do what I can. I need to be on the ranch. I'll go ahead and make some inquiries and be there in a couple of days. Tell the men that you have hired a manager. That will be my cover story, and give me an opportunity to go over the whole place without anyone being suspicious."

"May I tell one man, Brownie, the foreman? He's been in the middle most of the time, right along with us. We trust him entirely."

"Okay, but no one else right now. If things change, then we will cross that bridge when we get there. OK?" Jim and Sue nodded.

"I will have to tell everyone something when I drive up in a different truck."

"Tell the truth. It's easier than remembering a lie. They need to be on their toes and watchful."

"All the men are armed. So are the women."

Mason laughed, "The only thing worse than an armed woman is two armed women. No slur intended, Sue."

"None taken, but don't come bursting into that house unless you want a load of buck shot. Irene means business."

Mason nodded. "I'll remember that. Be careful and have a safe trip home."

"Good bye".

As they started driving, Jim asked Sue if she was satisfied with what they had accomplished that day.

"Yes. But what if they have been watching us today? Going from one place to another? Think they will try something on the way home?"

"I don't know. I guess we will have to keep an eye out and not let anyone get too close. Do you want to get something to eat or wait till we get back?"

"The only place is that truck stop where we had pie and coffee. Are you leery of stopping there?"

"I want to stop. I'm hungry. I'm going to get a cell phone tomorrow. I have never had one before but I could have used one several times lately."

"You can get one at the truck stop, if you want to, or wait until tomorrow." Sue told him.

"I want to get it tonight, and I also want to pick up a CB radio. Those truckers saved our lives today. I don't know if I could have held that truck through another hit. We could as easily have gone over the side instead of under that trailer. It's been a long time since anyone cared about me." Sue just nodded. When they got to the truck stop, they found a seat, ordered and then went to find a cell phone and a CB. Jim got both. The radio would have to be installed later, when his truck was repaired and returned to him. They ate their meal.

Jim asked for Sue's phone so Irene would recognize it when it came up on caller ID. Jim told her they had had some trouble but were alright. He told her where they were, and about how long it would take to get home, adding that if they didn't show up on time, to "send out the troops".

When Irene hung up, she was worried. "Send out the troops! I'll call out the Sheriff, the Highway Patrol and the National Guard to start with." She got busy in the kitchen to pass the time. When Jim hung up the phone, he gave it back to Sue.

"Let's go home."

She looked at him. "Does it feel like home to you?"

After they had looked at each other for a long time, he said, "It's beginning to."

"Good. Let's go."

Chapter 7

WHEN THEY GOT back, every light in the house, the bunk house and the cook shack was on. The men came out of the bunkhouse, Cookie from the cook shack. Jim told them to come on into the house. After he relayed all that had happened, the men were very angry, but didn't say a word. He told them that he and Sue had hired a manager who would be arriving in a day or two. Jim told the men to keep guards on duty at all times. They didn't know what to expect next. Again, he asked if anyone wanted to leave. No one did.

"With the failed attempt today, they will probably try again. That's all, men. Good night. Brownie, stay just a minute, please."

Jim took Brownie into the office. "Brownie, the manager is a Federal Marshal. He'll be trying to help us figure this out."

"I'm glad you brought the law in. I'll help all I can but I don't know if it will be enough. You sure can use his help."

"Keep it to yourself for now. If things change, I'll tell the men."

"Okay. Good night, then." Brownie left for the bunkhouse.

Sue fell into bed exhausted, but her mind continued to run long after she should have fallen asleep. She thought about all the events that had transpired not only during the day but throughout the weeks leading up to it. Sue realized she had come to depend on the fine brave man who seemed willing to risk his own life to help her, as she finally settled into a restless sleep.

Jim was also thinking about the events of the day, struggling to reconcile whether he should disclose everything he knew. He knew that both he and Sue were in danger, and he had developed an admiration for her ability and determination to solve the problems they were facing. He fell asleep hoping to avert a tragedy and debating possible actions he could take.

The next morning, Jim met the men to talk to them about what was on his mind.

"Things have gotten a whole lot worse and more complicated. I can't explain a lot right now, but we need to be on high alert. Again, if any of you want to leave, I'll understand."

The men shook their heads, Billy spoke for all the men, "I like working here. Not many bosses care about their men. They don't worry whether they'll get hurt or not. I'll stick with you, and wear my gun at all times." The others nodded agreement.

"You're good men and I think we have a damn good crew. Now, Cookie, you need to pick out your bed, anything as long as it isn't too expensive." Cookie had a big smile and said a twin bed would suit him just fine.

"I'll get Sue to get you linens, blankets and such things. Is the stove going to be warm enough or do you need a heater?"

"The stove will do fine for heating and I'll keep it going for coffee for the men changing guard duty."

"That sounds good. Brownie, the men need to circle the cattle and make sure they're alright. Keep that guard on duty at all times."

"Okay. Let's go, men."

Jim returned to the house and told Sue to gather some things for Cookie when he got his bed, as the cook shack was almost finished. Jim told Brownie he wanted the old cook shack to be torn down. Brownie said he would have the men get started the next morning. As the men gathered in front of the bunk house, Jim asked if they needed any supplies. Were they cold? Did they have enough blankets? Were the shower, washer and dryer working properly? The only thing they said they needed was more wood for the bunkhouse and cookhouse stoves. New to the place, Jim asked where they usually got the wood. Brownie told them that they got it from the woods behind the barn, and would start cutting and hauling the winter supply pretty soon. Otherwise, everything was okay.

The next morning, they were up early. It promised to be another beautiful day. The mountains with their snowcaps always fascinated Jim. He never got tired of looking at their majestic beauty.

Mason arrived about nine o'clock, in a dirty truck, not a late model. Jim had an idea that under that hood was an engine that could cover a lot of ground if needed, and would not be easily caught. Jim introduced him to Irene and showed him to his room. Mason said he wanted to look at all the paper work they had found and collected. He spent several hours in the office with Jim and Sue.

Jim explained to Mason that even though the men were armed, including Cookie, they were riding in pairs, watching each other's backs. Mason wanted to meet all the men. When the hands came in from the barn, the guard accompanied them, despite the fact that he hadn't been seen all day.

Jim introduced Mason to everyone as the new manager. He liked the looks of the men and they liked his looks, too.

"Keep the guard on duty, stay alert, no smoking."

"Jim's already told us that."

"Good. I am just reminding you, then. Jim and I need to take a ride tomorrow, so we'll be out on the range. Good night, men."

"Good night."

Jim and Mason went into the house, washing up before settling down to one of Irene's delicious home-cooked suppers.

Mason patted his stomach. "Irene, if you feed like this, I'll have to spend all my time out riding just to keep the weight off. That was some good food." Irene smiled back at him with sparkling eyes.

Jim, Sue and Mason returned to the office.

"Where's that oil sample report? I want to look at it again." Mason studied it for an hour or so. He said he was going to bed. It had been a long day.

After he left, Jim made a suggestion. "Sue, what do you think of drilling one test well? If there is oil, you could use the money to make improvements on the property. If they come in on the County road, they won't ruin your grazing land. You will lose the hay field, though. What do you think?"

Sue thought for a few minutes. Jim liked the fact she didn't make sudden decisions, but thought them through.

"If they come in by the County road, I would do it."

"Sounds good, we'll work out the details later. Say, have you found anything else on the computer or in the paper work?"

"No, I haven't. I don't think there is anything more. I've checked everything Dad did, it's just not there."

"Darn, maybe Mason will find some clues we've overlooked. We'll have a long day tomorrow, let's hit the hay."

Chapter 8

THE NEXT MORNING, Tommy brought the fridge, freezer and Cookie's bed. They moved everything to the new cook shack, then started tearing the old one down. They would be able to burn some of the wood for heat.

Sue brought the bedding down for Cookie. He was almost in tears. No one had ever done so much for him. He would spend the rest of his days here if possible. He was coming to love the ranch and all the people on it. Now, Cookie had two fridges and two freezers so he wouldn't have to go in to town and restock as often. Jim settled up with Tommy, pleased with his fast work.

Jim was watching Mason as Sue saddled up Red and got ready to ride out to the pasture. Mason didn't say anything as he watched her. They mounted up and rode out past the herd a little ways, before letting their horses have their heads and run. Red took off like he had wings. Mason and Jim just watched horse and rider.

Mason looked at Jim. "I've never seen a woman ride a stallion, but she sure can ride him. He is some horse."

"I'm trying to get her to use him to sire some colts. She can train them before she sells them and make good money. You know she raised Red from a colt and trained him."

Mason smiled. "I'm putting my name in the hat now. I want the first colt. He is a beautiful horse. We better go catch up to her now." They pick up a little speed and soon met her cooling Red down by letting him trot a little.

"Jim was telling me you may use Red to sire some colts. I'd sure be interested in buying the first one."

Sue let out a delightful laugh. "I'm still thinking about it but I'll put your name on the list."

"How much farther is it to the boulders?"

"Just over that hill."

When they reached the spot, they dismounted and Mason started circling the boulders. Just as Jim had done, he kept looking, and circling farther out with each circle. Jim kept glancing around, keeping alert for anything out of place, when a flash caught his eye. He didn't know whether it was from a gun or glasses, but he eased over to Sue, getting between her and the flash. The two of them slowly walked over to where Mason was.

Jim leaned over as though he was looking at the ground and said, "Don't stop what you're doing but I caught a flash from something."

"Is there any protection around here, Sue?"

"No, but if we work ourselves over that way, we will be out of his line of sight. Let's get the bastard! I'm tired of everything going their way." Sue said angrily.

Mason laughed, "Lead the way." They mounted and nonchalantly walked the horses along until they would be hidden, before spurring their horses.

Jim knew where the vehicle tracks were and figured this one would park in the same spot. They galloped part way then slowed them down to a quick trot.

Sue was the first to catch sight of the man as he was trying to get his truck started. He tried to run, but Sue and Red didn't give him a chance. They kept him in one place until Mason took charge of him.

Mason tied him with his rope, without speaking a word as he did so.

"He doesn't have an ID on him. I do have a friend that wants to talk to him." Mason laid the man across his horse across the back of the saddle, tying him with the strings that hung from the side, then rode back to the boulders. Jim watched their guest while Mason continued his search. He found the odd marks, looked at them a few minutes, then pulled a camera out and took pictures. They rode back to the ranch house slowly as Mason's horse was carrying double. When they rode up, all the men were there. They did not look happy when they saw the guest.

"Any of you know this man?"

"No Sir."

They dismounted.

"I need to take our guest to see my friend. He'll be ready to talk soon." Mason winked at Jim where the guest couldn't see him.

"Don't I get a phone call?" He asked. He was worried.

He knew he was in trouble.

"No, you are a guest and not under arrest, so no call. Jim, let's search his pockets thoroughly. We don't want a cell phone, tracking device, or something else left on him." They searched him up and down, even taking off his shoes. He didn't like it but there wasn't much he could do about it. Mason loaded him into his truck, said he would be back later and left. Sue unsaddled and brushed down the horses before going to the house.

Jim went over to talk to the men, "Brownie, I want you to take one man and bring in a truck that's parked out there where we saw tracks. Put it in the barn, cover it with a tarp, and cover that with hay. We don't want it seen. Men, keep a watch when you're out checking cattle. We caught this guy today because I was paying extra attention and looking around. I saw a flash, a scope, binoculars, glasses, I didn't know, but luckily it caught my attention. That may be the only warning you get. Keep a close eye on each other's back. Fire your gun three times if you run into trouble and we'll be there as fast as we can. I guess that's all." Jim went into the house.

Brownie and Dingo saddled up and rode out. A short time later, Brownie rode in leading Dingo's horse. Dingo drove the pick up into the barn. When Mason showed a couple of hours later, Jim looked at Sue and she nodded.

"Mason, Sue and I are thinking about having a test well drilled. That may bring these people out of hiding.

What do you think?"

Mason was silent a few minutes. "I think that's a good idea. I have a friend who is a wildcatter. Let me call him."

"Good news. He'll be here tomorrow about nine a.m. His name is Don Thomas and he'll bring a truck without the company name on it in case anyone is watching."

The next morning, Jim went into the barn to make sure the men completely camouflaged the truck. Jim gave Brownie his orders.

"Keep one man on guard duty, stay out of sight as much as you can, and no smoking. Ride carefully, men." The men saddled up and headed out to check the cattle and water.

Jim went back into the house. Just as he, Sue, and Mason, finished breakfast, Don Thomas showed up. He was driving a dirty truck and looked like a cowboy. Mason made the introductions. They sat around the table and talked while Don looked through the oil sample report. He studied it for a long time. The others waited, enjoying Irene's strong morning coffee.

"You have oil here alright. I want to see where they took the sample. My security team will go in ahead of everyone else. Do you want to drill a test well?" Don inquired of Sue and Jim.

"Yes, and you do understand that there may be trouble?" Sue replied worriedly.

Don grinned, "My security team will handle that."

"There's just one more thing. We want you to come in to the pasture from the county road so you won't ruin as much grazing land. Will that be a problem?"

"I'll know more after looking at the site."

Jim nodded. "Let's mount up." They went out to the barn to saddle the horses. Jim and Mason both watched Don as Sue saddled up Red. Red kept bumping her with his head, looking for another sugar cube. Don showed his surprise and looked at Jim and Mason.

Mason grinned. "Wait until you see him run!" They led the horses out, mounted up and rode out. They went past the herd before Sue flew past on Red, almost lying on his neck.

Don shook his head. "That's a first for me, but he is a beautiful horse and they are quite a pair."

"Sue raised him from a colt and trained him, they simply love each other. She may use him for a sire. I'm trying to talk her into it." Jim informed Don.

Mason smiled. "I've already got my name on the list. If she uses him, I want a colt."

"I think I'll put my name on that list, as well." Don mused. By then, Sue had slowed Red and brought him back to them.

Don grinned. "Add my name to your list. If you decide to use Red for a sire, I'll buy a colt." Sue just laughed.

Shortly they were at the hay field. Jim showed Don where the sample had been taken.

Don looked at the surrounding area. "I can see why you want to come in off the County road, it won't be a problem. You have good land here. Do you want me to move my equipment in? All of my men can be at the ranch house tomorrow. They need to see and meet all your men so they will know them. The security team is first on site. I'll be bringing a water tanker to control the dust."

Jim was worried. "Let's go back to the ranch before we discuss this anymore. I don't like leaving the ranch with only one guard, Cookie, and Irene."

Don agreed. "Let's go."

They settled around the table to talk. Irene served coffee and hot peach cobbler with ice cream. They all groaned with satisfaction, thanking Irene for the good food.

"Now, Don, all the men are armed, and Cookie has a gun strapped on. There is one guard on duty at all times. Sue and Irene are armed with pocket pistols, even while in the house."

"That's good. Sue, can you move that herd to a different pasture? They could stampede them through here and the ranch could be taken over during the confusion." Don pointed out.

"Yes, there's another pasture. Jim, Brownie knows where it is. We don't use it much as it makes it too hard to feed the herd in the winter. Makes for a lot of extra work but it will work for now. We can move the herd back after this is settled, hopefully, before bad weather sets in."

"I'll tell him tomorrow. Do we need a guard there, Sue?"

"Ask Brownie what he thinks about that, I'll leave that up to him."

"Do you want that test well?" Don questioned Sue and Jim.

"Yes. Let's see if we can smoke these men out. They will most likely get very upset when they see the equipment coming in. They'll know that we know about the sample." Sue told Don.

"In just that area that we looked at, you could most likely put in two wells. I'm sure there's oil there."

Sue shook her head, "Let's get the first one going before we see about the second one. I don't need all that much money, but I will use it to make improvements to the ranch."

"Okay. My men and equipment will roll in tomorrow. About that water, do you have a place I can fill the tanker?"

"Do you want just plain water or drinking water?"

"We haul in cases of bottled water for drinking. The tanker will be used for showering and cooking and will be full when we get here, but we'll need to refill it periodically. We have a generator for power to operate everything. We are mostly self-contained."

"When they get here tomorrow, Brownie can show

the tanker driver where the creek is for the "dust" water." Sue commented to Jim.

"Okay. Are there any other questions? No? I guess that takes care of that."

Don was walking out the door. "I'll see all of you tomorrow."

"Do you want to stay the night?" Jim offered.

Don shook his head. "Thank you, but I can't. I've got a lot to accomplish tonight to get my help and equipment ready to move here tomorrow."

"Alright, I guess we will see you in the morning."

Mason's phone rang and he walked into the office for privacy.

He came back into the kitchen shaking his head. "Our guest didn't have much to say. He couldn't or wouldn't identify the man that hired him. He was supposed to keep a lookout and wait at a certain phone for the man to contact him. When he didn't make contact, they probably realized that he was captured. Now we will just have to wait to see what's next."

When the men came in, Jim met them. He told Brownie about moving the herd and that he needed to be on the ranch the next day.

"No problem. I can do that. I'll give the men orders to move the herd. We may need to post a guard there."

"That's going to spread you men mighty thin."

"We don't have to be on the range so much now so

we can handle it." Brownie knew the men would handle whatever came up.

"Bring all the men in early. We have guests coming and they need to meet them."

"Okay." Jim did not explain and Brownie did not ask.

"See you in the morning. Good night." Jim went into the house.

Chapter 9

EARLY THE NEXT morning, Jim met with Brownie and the men. One man was to stand guard and Brownie would also stay close to the buildings. The other men were to move the herd into the other pasture and return. About noon time, a long line of trucks, tankers, trailers, pickups, and equipment, pulled into the yard.

Jim introduced the men. "Brownie, meet Don Thomas. He's going to drill a test well out in the hay field. Don, this is Brownie, the ranch foreman." The men shook hands.

Don called a man forward and introduced him. "Jim, Brownie, meet Tom Jacobs, my head security man." They shook hands. All the men introduced them-selves to Dingo, who had come out of the barn by now. Don's men were told that all the ranch hands were armed, including the cook and the women. The men grinned, agreeing that they didn't want to risk making the women mad.

"Brownie, you will need to show the tanker driver where the creek is. He needs to fill up, no drinking water in this tanker, dust control only."

Brownie nodded. "I can do that. Are you ready to go now?"

"Better not, we need to meet and see the other men, so we don't make any mistakes."

"They should be here soon. I told them to return as soon as possible." Meanwhile, Irene and Sue served coffee and slices of apple pie.

Just then the first silhouettes of the hired hands started appearing on the horizon. They came over for introductions, each man looking the others over so they would know them when they met again.

Brownie climbed into the truck with the driver to show him where to go.

Don and his men turned around and headed down the ranch road. The driver brought Brownie back and followed the other vehicles.

Jim asked the men how their morning had gone. They hadn't encountered any trouble while moving the herd, but thought it would be wise to post a guard. Jim told Brownie to set it up any way he wanted to. The men could change often so it would not be hard on any one of them.

"I'll take care of it. That pasture would be hard to stampede the herd out of. The trail is very crooked, that's why we don't use it much." Cookie rang the triangle and Jim went into the house.

Mason wanted to look at the aerial map again. Sue got it for him just as Irene called them to dinner. After they had eaten, Sue helped Irene clear the table. Mason was on his phone outside. Jim and Sue went into the office to talk.

"Jim, do you think we're doing the right thing with

the test well?"

"Yes. I do. We have to smoke these men out. When they see the test well going in, they will know we figured out what was so valuable on the ranch. They will have to make a move to keep us from getting the oil. After the well comes in, it will be too late to try anything. But I want to know who it is. I believe they killed Hawk and they made a damn good try at us. With us gone, the ranch would be up for grabs. We don't know what they will try next."

Sue's eyes filled with tears. Jim pulled her into his arms and held her. After a while, she pulled back, and smiled up at him. He bent his head and gave her a light kiss on the mouth. She said "good night" and went upstairs. Jim listened, lost in thought, as Mason climbed the stairs.

Chapter 10

AFTER BREAKFAST, JIM, Brownie, and Mason rode out to the well site. They met with Don to look everything over.

Don grinned, "We have a friend checking us out."

"Are you going to take care of him?"

"Oh, yeah. Hang around a little while." It wasn't too long until they saw three men coming.

"Who do we have here?" Don asked one of the men.

"He doesn't have any ID on him, nothing else either. What do we do with him?"

"I have a friend that would just love to have a chat with our guest. Tie him up and toss him over the horse. We'll take real good care of him." Mason smiled. Don's men just laughed as they secured their guest and put him on Mason's horse. The men rode slowly back to the ranch.

"Don't I get a call?" Like the other man, he was worried, knew he was in trouble.

Mason just shook his head. "No. You're just our guest and not under arrest. I have a friend that wants to talk to you." They had just ridden up to the barn when Dingo came out.

Something in the way Dingo glanced at their guest made Mason curious. "Do you know him?"

"No Sir."

Sue and Irene came hurrying out of the house. "Jim, Cookie went to town for supplies hours ago. He's never gone this long. We're afraid something has happened to him."

"Take good care of our guest, Dingo."

"My pleasure, go on and look for Cookie, we'll be right here."

The three men jumped into the truck and headed down the ranch road. Before they got to the turn off, they saw Cookie's truck in the ditch. Jim stopped and they jumped out and ran over to see what was wrong.

"He's in here. He's been knocked out." Brownie shouted, his concern evident. Cookie looked too pale.

Jim pointed to the truck. "Look, bullet holes. Someone shot up his truck, hit a tire and it blew. Is he bleeding anywhere that you can see?"

"No, but I'm afraid to move him. He may have broken bones."

Mason asked, "Do we need to call the EMTs?"

"No, we don't have EMT services, this town is too small. We'll have to call Doc." Doc arrived about twenty minutes later. He looked Cookie over the best he could in the cab.

"No broken ribs, but bruised. He is going to be sore and stiff after this rough ride. Lay him out flat in the bed of the pickup."

Once he'd been moved Doc was able to conduct a more thorough exam of Cookie. "I think it's safe to take him home. He's going to be in quite a bit of pain and will have a headache. He's most likely got a small concussion. Here is some medicine for pain if he needs it. Drive slow and careful to get him home."

"Thanks, Doc. We appreciate you coming out here." Jim told the doctor. He was worried about Cookie, also.

Doc replied, "No problem. Let me know if he has any trouble."

"Okay. See you later. Look, he fired his gun, so he got a shot at who did this. Let's load up the supplies back here with him and get him home. I will have his truck towed to a repair shop." When they drove in the yard, all the men were there and very worried. Sue and Irene hurried into Cookie's bedroom to turn back the covers. It was clean and neat as could be. Cookie took pride in his new bedroom. After turning back the covers, they left so the men could get Cookie ready for bed.

As they were pulling the covers up, he began to come around. He looked about him, surprised at all the men standing around.

"How are you feeling, Cookie? Do you have any pain? Doc left some medicine for you if you need it."

Cookie shook his head and muttered, "Give me a minute. I can't think straight right now."

"Sorry, I was rushing you. I didn't mean to do that.

Take all the time you need. We are just concerned."

Cookie was quiet for a few minutes, and then began to talk. "I was coming home from getting the supplies. After I turned onto the ranch road, a large black pickup pulled up alongside of me. They tried to run me off the road. That's been tried before with no success. Then they rolled down a window and pointed a gun at me, so I pointed mine right back at them. That sure surprised them. Then they backed off, and that's when they started shooting at the truck. I slammed on the brakes and they had to come up by me to keep from rear ending me and I got off a few shots at them. They backed off a little. I don't think they were expecting me to shoot at them. They started shooting again and finally hit a tire. I lost control of the truck then, I just couldn't hold it. That's all I remember."

"Did you get a look at them?"

"They were older men, not in their twenties, I mean. They were wearing black hats and sunglasses. I can't tell you much more. I was busy driving the truck."

"That's okay. Do you need some pain medicine? Doc said you most likely have a small concussion. You need to stay in bed for today, at least. See how you feel tomorrow. The fresh and frozen things have been put away. Don't worry about anything. I had your truck towed to a repair shop. Dingo, can you fix a meal for the men tonight?"

Dingo grinned, "Yep, but it won't be like Cookie would fix." The men laughed and filed out of the cook shack. When they got outside, they were sending their guest some very dirty looks. He cringed and cowered, still unsure of what would happen to him.

Jim went out to the men. "Well, today you have been able to see a sample of what we might run into here. Does anyone want to leave now? Brownie, I think we need two guards on duty around the clock. That's going to make it harder on you men."

"We will handle it." Brownie looked at the men and they all nodded.

Jim was getting frustrated as he couldn't seem to get a handle on what was going on with the ranch. He was really worried. "There's another truck parked out there now, get it and bring it in."

Brownie was watching Jim. "Dingo and I will go. Give it time some time Jim, I know it's frustrating, but we will all work together to get to the bottom of this." Brownie and Dingo left to get the truck.

"Jim, be patient. I'm taking our guest to my friend to see if he can answer some questions. Be back later tonight." As Mason drove off with the guest, Jim went into the house and told the women what had happened.

Jim was worried about their safety. "Sue, you and Irene be extra careful, I don't know what they'll do next. Keep your guns handy at all times."

Irene put dinner on the table and they sat down to eat. She fixed a plate for Mason and put it in the oven to keep warm. When he returned a couple of hours later, Irene warmed up his dinner and he ate. They were all exhausted and soon called it a day.

The next couple of days were fairly quiet, almost lulling them into a sense of security. Cookie had remembered one more thing he wanted to pass on to Jim. There was a decal on the door. He'd seen it before but couldn't remember where or what it was. It was too small to be an eagle when Jim asked about that.

"Let me think on it, eventually it will come to me."

It was about three o'clock in the morning when all hell broke loose out in the ranch yard. A truck had crept up the ranch road with the lights off, almost to the house, before it sped up and fired shots everywhere. They got more than they bargained for. All the men let loose, almost at once, firing shots right back at the pickup. The driver swung the truck around, made a turn, and tried to escape, but didn't get far Jim and Mason jumped in the ranch pickup, with men hanging on everywhere, and went down the road. They found the truck but the men were gone, they had escaped in the dark. It wasn't a black truck, although in the dark it was hard to see. Mason said he would look it over in the daylight and try to trace it.

"I think they got a warmer welcome than they were expecting."

Mason grinned. "We sure made it hot for them." When they got back home and went in the house, they were met by Sue with a rifle in her hands and Irene with a shotgun in hers.

"Whoa!" said Mason and raised his hands.

Irene said, "NO ONE is taking over this house."

Sue said, "NO WAY, JOSE." Mason and Jim just grinned. The women put the guns where they were easy to get.

Mason commented, "I would not want to be the man that tried to take over that house."

"Me either," muttered Jim.

As it was too close to daylight to back go to bed, Irene made coffee and started preparing breakfast. The sun was just rising and the day promised to be a beautiful one. The sun on the snowcapped mountain tops was awesome. Jim never got tired of looking at those mountains. He kept hoping to see the eagle again. When the food was ready, Irene set it on the table. After eating, Jim and Mason went out to meet the men.

"For your information only, Mason is a Federal Marshal. He will take charge of the pickup and have it examined. It will be transported in one of our enclosed trailers so people won't know what it is. Everyone will have to be on the alert. This is at least three attempts to harm us. Seeing that test well going in, they know we figured out what's on the ranch worth killing for. Apparently, killing means nothing to them. You're a good crew. I don't want to lose any of you so be extra careful. Keep that guard on duty at all times, with two guards at night. Does anyone want to leave?"

Dillard looked at all the men, they nodded. "We've found a home here. We'll defend it."

"Do you have any questions for Mason?"

"No Sir."

Mason stated, "I need a trailer, the largest one you have."

Brownie spoke up, "I'll show you where it is and help you load the pickup."

"Thanks."

"Do we need to check on the drilling crew?"

Mason shook his head. "No. Don has his own security team and they will protect his men and equipment. Let's go get the trailer, Brownie." After Mason left with the pickup, Brownie returned to the bunkhouse.

"Sue, do you want to take Red out for a ride and take a look at the drill site?" Sue agreed in a hurry. She was getting cabin fever. She was used to riding every day. They went out to the barn and Jim asked Brownie to ride with them. They let the horses run for a little while and then cooled them down. The drill site was a busy place, the rig was already up.

Don came over to them, "We heard a little gun fire early this morning, what happened?"

Jim told him about the warm welcome that greeted their night visitors.

Don laughed. "Good. They won't try that again. Maybe Mason can get a handle on things now. He's a good man. We haven't had any more guests pay us a visit. We keep an eye open at night so they won't try to blow up my equipment. My security team takes care of that. It shouldn't be too long before we have a well in. You have lost your hay field so think about placing that other test well over there. The equipment is already here, let me know what you decide to do, okay?" Jim and Sue nodded.

Brownie was looking at the set up and commented, "I'm impressed. Everything is neat and clean as it can be. And you aren't tearing up meadow you don't need. I've seen some drill operations that ruin the whole area."

"That's not me. I like to keep it as natural as possible. We have to do some damage, but we keep it as minimal as we can."

"I can see that."

Jim looked at Don. "Where are your security men?"

Don laughed, "Oh, they're around. You aren't supposed to see them." They all laughed.

"Well, I don't see them so that's good. We'll talk to you later."

They turned their horses and headed back to the ranch house. They rode up to the barn, dismounted, and tended to the horses. Brownie went to the bunkhouse, Sue went inside the house, and Jim went to check on Cookie.

"How are you doing, Cookie?"

"I'm doing fine. Just a little stiff and sore but that will go away. I want another chance at those two men. I'll teach them a lesson they won't forget for a long time. Do you think that was them last night?"

"I don't know. It wasn't a black truck. Let's hope Mason can find out some things from the truck, like finger prints."

Cookie grinned, "It got a little hot around here for them, didn't it?"

Jim laughed, "Yeah, it got a little hotter than they expected. All you men did a good job letting them know they weren't welcome. Take it a little easy until you feel good again. Your truck should be ready in a day or two. It will be delivered to you."

"Okay. You didn't have to do that, but thank you." He slapped his pistol and said they would keep watch.

"You don't want to come busting into the house or you're likely to get a load of buck shot."

"None of the men would do that. They know the women have guns and the only thing worse than a woman with a gun, is two women with guns. We all want to stay alive."

Jim laughed and headed to the house. Mason made it back in time for dinner.

Mason said their guest didn't know any more than the other one did. His friend would keep them as his guests to keep them from talking to anyone.

"There WERE fingerprints in the truck and we are trying to run them down. Also, there was a little blood so one of the men got nicked. Not enough to stop or slow him down, but it would remind him how hot it got on the ranch when they tried to shoot it up. Was there any damage?" Jim said none he could find. Mason said he was going to bed. It had been a long day.

Jim and Sue went into the office.

"When do you brand the calves and cull what you want to sell? And when is the sale?" Jim questioned Sue.

"We would already have branded the calves by now. I have been slow doing it because of the risk to the men. We cut out what we want to sell, and keep the rest. Sales are every Thursday."

"Can we do what needs to be done where they are now?"

"We can brand the calves there. The culls can be driven back to the home pasture and taken to the sale barn the next day, Wednesday."

"Let's get that done."

Sue grinned, "While we're at the sale barn, let's look at the mares, see what we find."

Jim smiled, "Okay."

Sue turned the computer on, logged in to the email account and a new message popped up. She opened it and then turned white. Sue was getting to the point where she didn't want to open any email messages. They were frightening her. Jim went around the desk to see what had upset her. The message read, "You won't keep the ranch. You may as well give it to me now."

"We'll show this to Mason in the morning."

Sue started crying very quietly, "Why are they doing this? We know about the oil now."

"They still want the wealth. Some people are just so greedy. I want to find the head man, he's the one I want." Jim pulled her into his arms and let her cry. After a while, she pulled away from Jim and just looked at him. Then she gave him a long kiss, said good night and went up to bed. Jim just stood there. Was Sue telling him something? He was starting to care for Sue more each day. His other life was fading away. It was hard to hold on to something that had been gone a long time. He would never forget his wife, Emily, entirely. They had been very happy. Jim was starting a new life here on the Six Killer Ranch. These thoughts and more went through his mind. After several minutes, he went upstairs, but once there he spent a restless night. He wondered how he was going to solve the problems on the ranch, and daydreaming of what his future could hold after he had.

Chapter 11

AFTER BREAKFAST, JIM talked to Brownie and told him what they had decided to do about the cattle. Brownie was all for it. They left two men on guard duty and the rest gathered the equipment needed and set out for the pasture. One day would handle the branding. They could separate the culls tomorrow, drive them to the home pasture, and transport them to the sale barn the next day.

There was other work that needed to be done, including getting started on the fire wood, but they were spread out kind of thin and the stress was taking its toll. No one knew the whole story or what they might run into next. The branding was finished by quitting time and they had a count on the calves. They got the equipment together and headed for home. Once home, they hung up the branding irons and put the stove away until it would be needed again. The men headed for the cook shack, Brownie headed for the house. He knocked on the door to report how many head they had done.

Sue had shown Mason the email message and he was trying to trace the sender's address. They went to join Jim when Irene called them to dinner. After the meal, they were sitting at the table drinking coffee.

"Mason. How did the man get dad's ID, or did he use

his own with dad's address and all? I had to show a picture ID before the oil man would talk with us."

"It had to be some one that knew him well. I would say he had a copy of your dad's driving license, imposed his own picture over it. In other words, a fake ID. How many close friends did your dad have?"

"He didn't have that many. There was the lawyer, of course, the banker, the manager at the sale barn. He drank coffee with a couple of men he had known all his life. That's about all. Mr. Ryder handled all his legal papers. The banker was just a banker. They were friendly but they didn't spend any free time just having fun or a cup of coffee. In fact, dad was on the ranch more than anywhere else. He loved this place. He struggled real hard to make a go of it. I was too young to help him then. He did most of it himself, along with the crew. The three old hands have been with him for years. He taught me everything to do on the ranch. He insisted that I learn it all so when he was gone, I could handle the ranch, and at least know if someone was cheating me. It broke my heart when he gave it to Jim. I understand now why he did. I could never handle this nightmare by myself."

"He was a smart man. He asked for help when he knew he needed it. We may not get the men for killing him, it would be too hard to prove now, but we will get them for attempted murder. I'm going to do some research on that lawyer. He looks like the most logical one to me. There are too many crooked lawyers in this country to suit me."

Mason left to work on his computer. Jim and Sue finished their coffee.

"Irene, you haven't had any time off in a while, do you want a half day?" Jim inquired.

Irene shook her head. "No. I'll take my time off when everything is settled back to normal. I'm not leaving Sue alone in this house. You men guard everything outside, Sue and I will take care of the house."

"Okay. Let me know when you want time off. Sue, do you still want to look at some mares?"

"Yes. I haven't changed my mind. We will take a look Thursday. We need Brownie to go with us. He knows his horses, too."

"Okay. I'll tell him in the morning. Do you need to do any more office work?"

"No. I'm done until we count the culls and sell them. We need to take care of the account at the store, too. Then we'll know how much money we have for a mare."

"I've hit your account pretty hard with the new cook house, freezer, fridge, and Cookie's bed. Are you okay with that? You have more men to pay."

"I'm fine with what you've done. The account can handle it. And what you've done is to make improvements to the ranch. With the extra cutting of hay, we will save on the winter feed bill, so it all works out pretty much across the board."

Jim nodded agreement. "Let's call it a day." They started for the stairs. Sue went into the office, turned out the lights and came out. Jim was waiting for her. He pulled her into his arms and kissed her. He whispered good night and let her go. Sue gave him a gentle kiss, said good night and climbed the stairs. Jim followed her, went into his room and closed the door. Sue showered and went to bed, and lay awake for a long time. She was falling for Jim King. She knew it and she felt like he was beginning to feel the same way. He was making The Six Killer Ranch his home. Her last thought before drifting off to sleep was a quick prayer that he would stay.

The next morning, the men went out to the pasture to begin the job of cutting out the cattle that Sue wanted to sell. Brownie knew how Hawk had always sorted, so that was the way he went about it. They drove the culls to the home pasture and got a count on them as well as the whole herd.

When they returned to the yard, Sue and Jim were waiting for them. Brownie gave Sue the counts so she could enter them into the computer records. Before she went into the office to work, she told them to load and haul them to the sale barn the next day. Jim told Brownie they wanted him to ride to the sale with them. Brownie raised an eyebrow in question. Jim laughed and said they were going to look at some mares that Red could breed.

Brownie smiled all over his face, "That's great! He will

be a great sire and his foals will be great, too."

Jim laughed at him, "I take it you approve of Sue's decision?"

"Oh, yeah, I do. Usually, there are a few mares at the sale. We may have to hit some auctions to get the ones we want." Jim said he and Sue figured the same thing but would check out what the sale had on Thursday, first. Brownie almost danced his way to the bunkhouse.

Chapter 12

THE NEXT MORNING, Jim met with the men, "Brownie, load the cattle in the trailer. I want you to drive that rig. Sue and I will leave out ahead of you. Leave the rest of the crew here to protect the ranch and the house. I'm expecting trouble today. Irene will be here alone so no guard on the herd today. Have two men in the barn, one in the bunk house and one with Cookie, close enough to help Irene. Mason will follow the rig. If we don't have any trouble today, it will be tomorrow when we're away from the ranch. Be careful, men. Keep plenty of ammo at hand. Try not to show yourself more than you need to. I'm expecting them to try to burn us out, so keep a close eye out. Mason and I will keep guard while you load the cattle. We will see you after breakfast."

Jim went back into the house. Irene put the meal on the table and they all sat down. Jim told them all what he had told the men. Jim asked Irene if she was okay with the plan.

"Yes. My shotgun is loaded and ready."

After they finished eating, Jim and Mason went with the men to the home pasture and stood guard while the cattle were loaded. Jim said the cattle looked good. Brownie drove the rig into the yard and parked it. When

Sue came out of the house, she had her pistol strapped on, as did Jim and Mason. Mason climbed into his truck. As Jim and Sue climbed into Jim's truck, he looked around. The ranch yard looked abandoned. Brownie and Dingo were in Hawk's pickup pulling the trailer. It was the best Jim could think to do. Jim and Sue led the way, Brownie next, and Mason last. It was about an hour ride to the sale barn. Brownie backed the trailer up to the loading docks, opened the doors and the cattle went down the ramp. Sue was standing with Mr. Simmons, the manager, counting the cattle as they came past them.

When they were satisfied with the count, Mr. Simmons told Sue, "I'm sorry about your dad. I knew him for a number of years. He was a good man. I'll deal as fair with you as I did with him."

Sue answered, "Thank you. And I know you'll deal fair with me. We'll see you tomorrow for the sale." They started the trip back home.

When they pulled into the yard, they knew something had happened. As they stopped the vehicles, the men came out of the buildings. They were trying to curb their excitement.

Jim looked at them. "Okay, men, what happened?"

Brazos stepped forward and told them, "Just what you expected. A truck with four men pulled into the yard. They all got out, the first man said, "You, set fire to the barn. You, set fire to the bunkhouse, and I'll take the house." We waited until the one was almost to the house, then let loose. We didn't try to kill any of them, just wound them so we could capture them. When the one close to the house turned to see what was going on, Irene let him have a load of buck shot in the seat of the pants. He sure did a lot of fancy dancing there for a few minutes. They all ran back to the truck and hauled ass out of here. We got the license plate number for you, Mason. It was a red extended cab Ford F450, about three years old.

They weren't shooting, so no one or nothing got hurt. We had a little fun and made it real hot for them." By the time Brazos was through, everyone was laughing. Mason said he would get right on that tag number. Jim told the men they had handled things really well. Sue went and shook hands with each man, said thank you. Brownie and Dingo backed the trailer into its parking place and unhooked it, then parked the truck.

All the men went into the cook shack. Jim, Sue and Mason headed for the ranch house.

Jim opened the door, called out, "Is it safe to come in?" Irene laughed and told them to come on in. There was coffee and pie on the table.

"Are you okay, Irene?"

Irene laughed. "I'm fine. I had some fun today. Mason, check with the doctors and hospitals. He'll have to have that buck shot removed from his butt. I could have killed him, I already had him in my sights, but I didn't want to do that. So I let him turn and then blasted away." Mason said that was the best way. Once you kill a man, it's hard to live with, even if he's a bad man. Sue gave Irene a big hug and wiped the tears away.

Irene commented, "We could have handled more men than was sent. How did you know, Jim?"

"It was just a guess. They must be keeping an eye on us. But they can't get a handle on how many men we have. I figured either they would try to burn us out or make a try on us with the cattle. When they didn't make a try at the cattle, it had to be the ranch. Now, tomorrow, they may come after us. When they find out that we bought a mare or two, if we can find any, they may try to take the mares out. We best make a trip to the drill site and let Don and Tom know we're all right. Mason, do you want to go with Sue and me?"

"No, I'm going to start tracing that plate number. And start calling doctors and hospitals. That man will get infection if the buck shot isn't removed."

"OK, I'll get Brownie to ride with us. They may try to take us out while we are out on the range with Brownie. But at least, someone will know what happened. They can't catch Sue on Red but they may try to take her out. If they take me first, she can out run them. Red will run until he drops, for her."

Sue was stunned, "Jim?"

"I'm just stating facts. Without us, the ranch is up for

grabs. I can't leave it to you, now, not with all the trouble and I won't risk another life. Sue, face the facts and it's easier to deal with."

Sue shook her head, "I'll try. I'm still dealing with dad's death, possible murder. Things seem to be piling up on me."

"We have a crew that will fight to the death for this ranch and for us. You can't get better than that." After that, Mason went up to get on his computer and start tracing the plate numbers.

Jim and Sue went to the barn. Jim called Brownie and asked him to ride with them. All three saddled and then led the horses from the barn, mounted up and rode out to the drill site.

Tom and Don met them.

"We heard shooting? What happened?"

The three of them laughed, "The only one hurt is the one with a load of buck shot in his butt." Then told them how it went down.

Don and Tom laughed and Don said, "I told you, you don't want to mess with an armed woman. We're glad none of your people were hurt. I'm glad they didn't try to kill those men, but things may get worse and you may have to change your mind on that."

"I know but I really don't want to do that. I would like to rope and drag THE BOSS, convince him to change HIS ways."

Sue was curious about the well, "How's that well going? You have kept things in good shape."

"We're down almost a thousand feet and it should be coming in soon. You will know when it blows, we can't stop that, but we will cap it real quick and put in a pump. Are you getting excited about it, Sue?"

"Not really. I will if and when it comes in, but right now, it just seems like one more problem. We will be at the sale barn tomorrow. We're going to be checking out some mares."

"That's great. Remember, my name's in the hat for a foal. Tom, you want to add your name?"

"Yes I do. That's a great horse that you're riding. He'll give you some good foals, Sue."

"If it works out, I'll be training his babies so that's going to make them more expensive."

"That's fine by me. You did a great job training Red, so it will be worth the extra expense." Brownie listened to the discussion with a huge grin on his face, excited at the prospect of working with his first love, the horses.

"Have you had any more visitors?"

"No. I'm letting some of my security team spread out and try to find out where these people are holed up, watching the ranch and house. They knew when you left but not how many men you left at the ranch. Tom, do you have anything to report to Jim?"

"No. I've got a couple of men checking some places

out. The 'well' comes first but I'm covering extra ground. If I find anything, I'll let you know." Tom told Jim.

"Okay. We'll head back home. See you later." The three of them turned and rode away.

"Jim, are you getting excited about the well coming in?"

"Not yet. There will be a lot to do after it comes in before you see any money. And the oil company has to be contacted and a deal made. Then you may see some money but at least you do know at that point that it will be here sooner or later. Brownie, you and Sue know this ranch better than anyone, where could those men be hiding and keeping watch on us? With binoculars or a scope, they wouldn't even have to be close. They can't keep up with how many men we have but they know what's going on. They'll know when we leave tomorrow. The men are going to have to be ready for a fight and this one may be a lot worse. Since burning the ranch didn't work, they may come in shooting and throwing bombs to set things afire and we can't fight fire. If they try that, shoot to kill."

Brownie nodded. "I'll talk to the men tonight and warn them what they may be up against. Dingo will be with them so that's another man. Let's talk to Irene about Dingo being in the house with her. If they capture her, our hands would be pretty much tied. We won't risk her life. We will risk our lives, but not hers. I'll think about places to watch from at a distance. Sue, do you remember any old line cabin from way back or some place your dad took you when you were too young to work the range? I know that he took you all over the property."

"I'll think back to those days and see what I come up with." Sue said thoughtfully.

Chapter 13

THEY RODE INTO the yard, dismounted, fed and brushed the horses. Brownie said he would talk to the men and update them on what to expect. Jim and Sue went into the house.

"Irene, we'll be gone to the sale tomorrow. There will be six men on the ranch and we are taking Brownie with us. Brownie suggested that you let one of the men be in here with you tomorrow. They're afraid that you might be captured and if you are, their hands will be tied. They are willing to risk their own lives, but not yours. Will you let one of them be in here with you? He can be in the upstairs front guest room. He would have a good view. We're expecting shooting and maybe some fire bombs."

Irene replied without hesitation, "Of course. Have Dingo or Brazos in here. They're the oldest hands. Between them and my shot gun, no one is going to take this house. The men may not risk my life but I will defend this house until I'm dead." Jim and Sue both had tears in their eyes. They each gave her a big hug.

Jim had trouble swallowing a lump in his throat. "I lost my mom a long time ago but I think I just found a second one. You have a home here as long as I'm here." Sue said the same thing. Now, Irene had tears in her eyes.

Jim wiped his tears away. "I'll go tell Brownie so he can set it up."

Brownie said he would let the men decide who would be in the house with Irene. Jim told him what Irene said about defending the house till death.

Brownie just shook his head. "That's one hell of a woman." The men grinned and nodded. Jim went back to the house

The next morning, Mason told them he had an ID on the plate number and it wasn't local. He'd also run the fingerprints and came up with a match. They were what you would call "bad men" but not local. He had BO-LOs out on both. They were closing in on answers, but it was slow work. Mason hoped to have more information before long. His friend was running down leads. No one had showed up at a doctor's office or hospital yet, but most likely would before long. His butt had to be giving him fits. If he hadn't been treated by now, infection was setting in and that would make him feel worse. Mason approved having a man in the upstairs front guest room while they were gone. Jim told him he told the men to shoot to kill if they tried to fire bomb the buildings.

Mason didn't blame Jim for giving the orders to protect the men, Irene, livestock, and property. "Alright, but remind them that they need to try to capture one of them, if they can't get all the men. We still don't even know who is behind the whole thing."

"Sue, do we need to take a trailer in with us, or do you want to wait and see the mares?"

"Wait on it. If we find a mare or some mares we like, Brownie and Dingo can go get them."

"Sue, Brownie should ride with Mason. If we have trouble, they can rescue us. What do you think Mason?"

"That's okay with me. I'll get Brownie and tell the men to capture at least one of the men, all of them, if they can. Do you have a way to shut down the road, if they come in?"

"Let Brownie talk to the men, they will figure out a way to shut it down. If nothing else, put a trailer across it when they come into the yard. Brownie, Brazos and Dingo will know the best place to put it. No one wants to run into a trailer." Jim told Mason as he went to talk to the men.

Jim and Sue got into Jim's pickup. Mason and Brownie got into Mason's and then they left. Feeling the power of the engine comforted Brownie, he knew they could get where they needed in a hurry if there was an emergency.

The remainder of the men gathered together in the cook shack to work out a plan.

Brazos explained, "I'll be in the house, upstairs front guest room. Dingo, hook the largest trailer to Hawk's pick up, stash it by the barn. Two men in the barn, two in the bunk house and one in the cook shack with Cookie. Here's our chance to get some of our own back. Don't risk your lives but give them hell. Dingo, after they come into the yard, you slip out the back of the barn and pull that trailer across the road. I think that's the best, do you agree?"

"Yep, that's the best place. We want to make sure no one goes in the house. We don't want Irene hurt. She can sure use that shot gun. Jim and Sue have entrusted us with the defense of the ranch and the ranch house. Let's do our best to keep them safe. If Sue lost Red, she would never forgive us. Do you men have any questions or comments to make? No? Let's go set it up and get ready for our guests. Because I feel sure they're coming."

The men did what they had to do. Brazos knocked and when Irene let him in, he went up the stairs to the front guest room. The men waited, and it wasn't a long wait. It happened just like Jim had feared. It was a short battle. With the trailer across the road, the men had no place to go and bullets were hitting all around them. They dropped their guns and their bombs. Three men covered them while three men tied them up. They lined them up in front of the bunk house and made them sit on the ground. Brazos called Jim and told him what happened. Mason was delighted to finally get some men that could tell him some things. He called his friend for a van to transport the men in. The enclosed trailer would be used again to move the truck. Mason could charge these men with attempted arson and attempted murder.

Mason inquired, "Do you have any trouble keeping an eye on them until we get back?"

Brazos replied, "No Sir. We can keep our guests entertained while we wait for you."

"Is the trailer still blocking the road?" Jim asked.

Brazos answered, "Yes, we haven't moved it yet."

"Don't. Leave it where it is. No one can come in and try to rescue those men. Keep your eyes open, they may try to sneak in on foot. Leave a man in the house with Irene. The rest of you keep out of sight."

"Okay. We will handle it."

Jim, Sue and Brownie were looking at the mares. There was only one they were interested in. They finally made a deal for her and Sue told Mr. Simmons they would be back tomorrow to pick up the mare and the check from the cattle sale.

They started back to the ranch. About halfway home, Jim's truck started to sound a little odd. Jim pulled over and they got out. Mason parked behind them and wanted to know what was wrong. Jim said the truck sounded funny. They walked off a few paces and stood looking at it to see if anything was dragging.

Jim said, "I'll raise the hood," and had taken one step toward it when the whole truck blew up. Everyone was knocked down. As Jim was the closest, he got more of the blast than the others. Sue, Mason and Brownie got up. Jim didn't.

Sue said worriedly, "Jim?"

Mason moved her aside and checked him over. "There are no broken bones, no burns, no bleeding, concussion, most likely. Call the Doc, Brownie. Let's get him looked at before we try to move him."

Brownie called the Doc. He was there in twenty minutes. He looked at the truck and shook his head. He examined Jim and said he thought he could be moved without hurting him. Brownie called Dingo and told him where they were and to come help. Dingo drove up a few minutes later, took everything in, and shook his head at what was left of Jim's truck. Dingo, Mason and Brownie loaded Jim in the back of Mason's truck. Mason drove slowly to the ranch house. All the men were outside and wanted to know what had happened.

To a man, they turned and angrily looked at the four prisoners and walked toward them. "Shall we make an example of these four? We can hang them from the barn."

Mason told them they couldn't do that. He would like to, but it was against the law and he represented the law. They carried Jim into the house and put him on the living room sofa. When he woke up, they would help him get upstairs and into bed. In the meantime, Irene and Sue were tending to him. Doc had given him some medicine to take for the pain. Sue told Irene if Jim had not stopped the truck when he did, they both would have been blown up. Some one was seriously trying to kill them. Irene gave

Sue a hug, said to hang in there, she had faith in Jim and Mason. They would solve the problem before too much longer.

Mason's friend showed up with a van and wanted every detail related to the explosion.

When Mason explained about the truck, he was angry all over again. "One of them will talk and be glad to do it before I'm through with him. I have just been playing around, now I get serious. Mason, help me load them up, then we'll need the longer flatbed to haul both pickups out of here. I'll go over every piece of Jim's to see what I can find. That bomb had to be placed there while all of you were at the sale. Talk to people, see what they can remember."

Brownie had the trailer hooked to Mason's pick up, then helped him load the one in the yard and followed him down to Jim's and helped load that one. They had to use a winch to load Jim's. The van and Mason left.

Brownie went back to the house, knocked and Sue answered.

"How's Jim? Is he awake yet?"

"Come in, Brownie. He's just coming around. You can help him upstairs and into bed." Jim was lying on the sofa with his eyes open but he was still about half out of it.

"Is everyone o.k.? No one else was seriously injured?"

Brownie answered, "You got the worst of it, Jim. Everyone else was knocked down, will be a little sore and stiff but not like you. You most likely have a concussion. Doc left you some medicine if you're in pain."

"I have a headache but it's not too bad. What about my truck?"

"It's a total loss. Mason took it to run some tests and see what they can find."

Jim smiled wryly, "I owe that dealer a truck. That was the loaner. My truck won't be ready for another day or two. I'll have to call him and tell him what happened. His insurance and my insurance may cover most of it."

"You can use Hawk's truck until yours is ready. Mason took the four men in a van driven by his friend. The men wanted to hang them but Mason wouldn't allow it." Sue explained.

Jim was worried about Sue's safety. "Sue, I want you to stick close to the house. Brownie, you and Dingo ride out to the well site and let Don, Tom and the crew know what happened. Then you and Dingo go into town and get the new mare and Sue's check from the sale barn. I don't think I'll be up to that trip. Now, help me upstairs so I can get into bed. I don't feel worth a damn."

Brownie grinned, "I can understand that. Come on, I'll get you to bed. Sue, bring a glass of water and some of that medicine Doc left for him in a few minutes. Let's go, pal."

Brownie got Jim upstairs and into bed. Sue brought the medicine and Jim swallowed the pills and promptly fell asleep.

Brownie went back to the bunk house. All the men were there except the guards. Brownie and Brazos drove out to the drill site and were met by Don and Tom. Brownie told them about the blast, and Brazos filled everyone in on what had happened in the ranch yard.

"We heard shooting earlier and then we heard the blast. These people are bent on killing Jim and Sue. How is he doing?" Don asked.

"He's doing alright, not great. He's sleeping right now, but he has a concussion as he was the closest to the truck when it blew. He should be okay in a few days, after he gets some rest. They are going to stay home while Dingo and I are going to get the mare they bought. She's a pretty thing. She'll be a good mate for Red."

About that time, one of the men on the rig yelled, "FIRE IN THE HOLE!" Don and Tom started moving back and told Brownie and Brazos to get out of the way. The men were running away from the drill rig. Then Brownie and Brazos felt the rumble deep in the ground.

"Here she blows!" Don yelled. Then the oil shot up hundreds of feet in the air. Brownie and Brazos stood there with their mouths open, it was a sight to see.

Don was laughing and grinning ear to ear, he yelled at Brownie and Brazos, "What do you think?" They just shook their heads. Don told them to get the cap on the well and his men got busy. Brownie and Brazos left to go back to the ranch and tell Sue and Jim their well was in.

When they rode into the yard, everyone was outside waiting for them.

"What was that noise?"

"That was the oil well blowing," Brownie told them, shaking his head.

"There is oil like you wouldn't believe. Don and his men were getting ready to cap it. You can't believe what it felt like under your feet when it rumbled, down in the ground. It was awesome! Sue, you have an oil well."

The exhilaration of hitting oil struck Sue like a bolt of lightning. She had looked over the papers and knew that it had affected Hawk's fate, but until she actually saw the oil, she couldn't quite believe it was real. She was not prepared for the rush of adrenaline, nor the tears of joy that streamed down her face.

There really was oil and there would be a lot of money from it. Her dreams of raising prize horses could be realized as well as Hawk's lifelong dream of breeding purebred Herefords. All their dreams could now become reality. The more she stood there, the larger her dreams grew, shaking her head she knew she wanted to share her enthusiasm and future plans with Jim.

Jim was also excited but was rather more practical about the whole situation, saying they needed to be certain that everything was in order legally before they told anyone outside the ranch.

"Now that the well is in, and these people know it,

they will most likely step up the task of getting rid of Jim and me. You men are going to have to be on your toes. Jim should be up and around tomorrow but not fit for much. Mason should be back some time tonight. But the burden rests mostly on you men. You have already done more than we can expect."

"We will stand as long as we're needed and then some. This is home."

"Thank you. You know what to do, Brownie, take care of it. Dingo, you and Brownie take the small trailer and get our new mare."

Dingo grinned, "Yes, Ma'am."

"And be careful. One of you should stay with the truck. We don't want another blow up." Dingo nodded. Cookie rang the triangle and all the men went in to eat.

When they sat down, Brownie told them, "Keep the guards on duty. Keep your guns handy, even when you sleep. Keep your eyes open. Use a trailer and block the road when Dingo and I leave in the morning. When we get close with the trailer and mare, I'll call and you can move the trailer. From now on, it stays across the road. Mason should be in before long. We need a couple of dogs to let us know when someone is around. Anyone know where we can get a couple of dogs?"

Cookie nodded and answered. "I do. I'll call the man and see when he can deliver them."

Sue took dinner upstairs to Jim. He was a little drowsy

but hungry. While he ate, Sue enthusiastically shared the news about the oil and what had happened at the ranch while they were gone.

He grinned at her, "That's good. Now, you will have to decide if you want the second one. You might as well. The men and equipment are already here. Like Don said, you've lost the hay field anyway."

Sue grinned, "I think I might go for it." Mason arrived and came up to check on Jim. Jim was just finishing his tray of food.

Mason asked, "How are you doing, Jim?"

"I'm doing okay, but Sue on the other hand is doing great, she has some big news." Mason looked at Sue.

"The oil well came in today. We have a gusher."

Mason grinned, "That's great news!"

"Yes. But I'm worried. Now they know for sure that there's oil here, I'm afraid they'll escalate their attacks, they're obviously trying to kill us."

Mason was thoughtful for a few minutes, "That's a possibility, but after today it's going to be harder for them to get men to do their dirty work. Six men have disappeared and two were shot. One a little, another with a load of buck shot. Bad men don't want to lose. When my friend gets through questioning this latest bunch, I may have a better lead. This last group of men are facing attempted murder and attempted arson. I hope at least one of them will want to make a deal. They'll be going down for a long time."

"Have you ever had a well blow when you were close?" Sue asked Mason.

"No."

"You need to talk to Brownie and Brazos. They were standing with Don and Tom when it blew. They were amazed at the rumbling and the sight. It will be worth a trip to the bunk house to talk to them."

Mason grinned. "I'll go down there now."

"I'll have to talk to them and get the story." Jim muttered to himself.

"Maybe tomorrow. Now it's time for your medicine and you get some sleep. Your head ache should be gone in the morning, and you can come down for breakfast. Good night." She leaned over and gave Jim a long kiss. Jim smiled at her, gave her a quick kiss and she was gone. Sue was relieved at Jim's recovery. He'd given her a real scare when she saw him lying on the road after the explosion.

The next morning, Brownie and Dingo hooked up the small trailer and headed to the sale barn. Dingo stayed with the rig, Brownie went in to see Mr. Simmons. He gave Brownie the papers for the mare and the check from the cattle. Brownie then got the mare and led her out to the pickup and trailer. She was a pretty horse and walked right into the trailer. They secured her and started for home. They didn't run into any trouble with this trip and when they neared the ranch, Brownie called ahead to have the trailer barricade moved so they could pass.

They unloaded the mare, and everyone took a look at her. Sue went up to her, talked softly and gave her a sugar cube. Brownie led her into a stall and brushed her down so she would get used to people handling her. She seemed to enjoy the attention. He gave her hay. He made sure the water was working, closed the stall door and came out.

Sue commented, "We will have to do something different when she comes in season. Red will go crazy, if we don't."

"You're right. We'll have to fix her up a place out of his sight and smell. We have a little time before that happens, according to her papers. Here are her papers and your check."

"Thanks. I'll put the information on the computer and set up a paper file for her. Her name on the papers is Lady Beauty. I didn't think to ask what it was at the sale yesterday."

"Sue, Cookie is trying to get hold of a man he knows who owns well-trained dogs. We need a couple to turn lose at night to let us know if someone is prowling about. Is that okay with you? I don't know what the cost will be."

Sue nodded, "That's fine. We should have had dogs on the place already. Hawk wasn't fond of them, as you know. We needed them a long time ago."

"I don't have too much information on them. I suggest we all get instructed in how to handle the dogs after they arrive here. They may be able to run free all the time."

"Let us know when he gets here. I expect Jim to be up and about tomorrow, but I don't think he'll be up for riding the bucking bull any time soon."

Brownie grinned and laughed, "No. I don't expect so. I'll see you tomorrow."

Sue nodded. "Good night, Brownie."

Sue went into the house and checked on Jim, who was still sleeping. Irene put dinner on the table for Mason, Sue and herself. Sue shared the news about the dogs with Irene and Mason. He agreed that it they would be beneficial. "Dogs will let you know if someone is around before you even think about it."

"Did you talk to Brownie and Brazos?" Sue asked.

"Yeah, they said it was awesome. They could feel in their feet when it started to rumble underground. I'll ride out there tomorrow and see it."

"I would love to go see it but Jim asked me to stay close to the house. Maybe we can ride out there when he's feeling better. He said he had to call that dealer and let him know what happened to his truck."

"I'll call him first. Jim can talk to him later. When is Jim's truck supposed to be ready?"

"In a couple of days," Sue replied.

"I have that truck. I'll talk to the dealer. When we get through with the truck, he can send his insurance adjuster to look at it, but it's a total loss. We have found out that there were two sticks of dynamite rigged with primer cord. There was some dirt in the fuel and it got caught in the fuel line, that's all that saved you two. Had both of you been in the truck, you would have been killed. I talked to Simmons at the sale barn and they don't have cameras set up. We know that's where they had to have rigged it. Simmons said nothing like this had ever happened before. I expect to hear from my friend either tonight or in the morning. One of those men is going to talk. If not, they're looking at a long jail time. Thanks for another good meal, Irene."

Irene shrugged and replied, "Thank you, it's all in a day's work, and I do enjoy cooking."

Sue helped clear the table and went into the office to do some paper work and enter information into the computer. She logged on to her email and a message popped up. She opened it and called Mason. He looked at the message. "You were lucky this time. Don't count on it the next time. Give up the ranch." It was a different sender's address this time. Mason said he would try to trace it down.

"You and Jim best stay close to home. These people are getting desperate. They have tried how many times and failed? They've lost at least six men, the two that were shot have probably quit. I'll be glad when those dogs get here. I'm going to work on my computer and then go to bed. I suggest you do the same, Sue. Try to get some rest.

I know this is hard on you, but hold on just a little longer. We will win." With that, Mason left.

Sue did her work, closed down the office and went upstairs. First, she checked on Jim. He was still sleeping. She took her shower and went to bed.

Chapter 14

THE NEXT MORNING, Jim came down for breakfast. He was sore, stiff and very careful about the way he moved.

Irene shook her head. "Jim, sit down before you fall down." They all laughed.

After they had eaten, Sue said, "Mason, can you get a chopper?"

Mason looked at her and said, "Why?"

Sue told Mason, "We need Brownie, will you ask him to come in here, please?" They waited until he was seated at the table, having coffee.

Sue looked at Brownie and said, "Do you think you could find that old mining cabin?"

Brownie looked surprised and said, "Damn."

Mason, "What's this about?"

"There's an old mining cabin up in the edge of the mountains. I don't know if it's on my property or not. But with good glasses, anyone up there would have a clear view of the ranch and house, including the oil well."

Brownie was stunned, "I haven't thought of that place in years. No one has worked that mine in at least twenty years. What made you think about it Sue?"

"I don't know. It just popped into my head last night

after I went to bed. It's too far to ride horses and a truck can't reach it, that's why I asked about the chopper."

Mason said thoughtfully, "I don't know. I have never asked for one before, I'll see what I can do."

"Jim, we got another nasty email last night. They said we were lucky this time but the next time we wouldn't be."

Brownie's face was grim, "Mason, if you get a chopper, I can lead you there. Don't know if we can land or not, it's been too many years to remember much. But I'll locate it for you. Now, I'm going back to the men. We will defend this ranch, with our lives if necessary." He left.

Sue was serious. "I think Brownie just got mad and he's slow to get mad but he's hell on wheels when he does. When he gets through talking to the men, I would not want to be the one that crosses them."

Jim nodded, "Are you going to ride to the well, Mason?""

"Yes."

"Be careful. They have figured out by now that you're the law. They may try to take you out. Take one of the men with you. Brazos is a good man to stand with."

"Okay. Now, I want to see if I rate a chopper," and grinned.

Suddenly there was a disturbance in the yard and a very frightened, upset man was escorted into the house by Brownie and Brazos, both of which had their guns on him with every step. Brownie explained that the man claimed to be a deer hunter and had found a man's body up in the timbered area near the old cabin.

Mason immediately decided to have Brownie and Brazos accompany him and the deer hunter to the site.

The hunter said they could get up there with four-wheelers. He had ridden his into the ranch, and there was another one, although rarely used, sitting in the garage. Mason rode with the hunter and the hired men took off on the other one.

Sue paced the floor, wondering who they would find up there. Would it be another hunter, one of the men trying to kill them, or someone else?

Hours slowly drug by, but finally they returned. Mason went into the office to arrange for a chopper, another officer, and the coroner to come out as soon as it was daylight to try to identify the body.

Brownie took Sue aside and told her that although he couldn't be certain, he was afraid they might have found Joe Purdue.

"Oh no, as soon as we know for sure I will have to go along when someone goes to tell Grace. That poor woman has had too much heartbreak in her life, and she and Joe have always been like family to Hawk and I."

The chopper was there at dawn and their worst fears were realized. Jim was feeling better by now and he took Sue into town to break the news to Grace.

Grace didn't break down but only said that those evil

men now had more than one death to answer for, as she was sure the same people had killed both her husband and Hawk.

Mason and the men went back up to the old claim shack which did show signs of having been recently occupied, but there was no way to know whether by hunters or the men who were causing all the trouble at the ranch. Mason thought that probably it was the evil-doers, but it appeared to have been recently vacated. He thought that with deer season in full swing they may have worried about being discovered.

Mason, Brownie, and Brazos returned to the ranch with hard set expressions, grimly telling Jim their suspicions that the shack had been used for surveillance of the ranch.

Sue walked in and told them that Grace was planning a memorial service for Joe, but was putting it off until things had calmed down at the ranch so they could all attend without worrying what might happen in their absence.

She also mentioned that her dad's lawyer, Mr. Ryder, had stopped by to offer his condolences, which surprised Grace who later remarked that she barely even knew him.

Cookie told them the man with the dogs would be there about five p. m. His name is Jackson, but everyone calls him Black Jack. He's a black man who trains dogs for the police departments and the military. He is a good man and his dogs are well trained.

When he arrived, he was driving a beat up truck, but the engine sounded powerful. There was no writing on the doors.

He asked everyone to come into the barn, "Under these circumstances, I didn't figure you wanted to advertise what's going on." He led the dogs into the barn, made a hand signal and they sat at attention.

"I name my dogs with odd names. This one is Andy, this one is Barney. The names are easy to remember. Is this everyone?"

"Everyone is here but Irene, the housekeeper, and Cookie. We didn't think they needed to know them."

"They need to meet them so they will have their smells. Get them, please." Dingo went to get Irene and Cookie. They came into the barn.

Black Jack pointed to the dogs. "Irene, then Cookie, I want you to pet the dogs and talk to them. That's Andy, this is Barney." Irene held her hand out and let them smell, she petted them and talked to them both. Cookie did the same thing.

Black Jack nodded, "Okay. That's all. They know you now and won't alarm any one if they meet you. Now, all of you do the same thing." It took a while but soon that was done.

"There are only hand signals, no voice commands. If someone is prowling around, they will come to one of the guards and let you know something is wrong. You'll learn to tell the difference when it is just friendly and when something is wrong. The hand signals are easy to learn, I'll leave you a sheet of paper that shows each one. In the day time, they will stay mostly in the barn. If you want them to circle the house and yard, just use the hand signals. They will be outside all night. Let them know who is on duty and where they are. If they find something, they will come get you and show you where it is. They won't attack as these dogs aren't taught to do that. I train some that do, but I don't think that's what you need here. I brought some food and their bowls. You will have to get more food in a few days. Don't feed them too much, makes them lazy. Like us when we eat too much, we want to lie down and go to sleep."

Jim suggested, "Come into the house and we'll settle up with you."

"No, try them for a week and see how they work out, then we'll discuss terms. Feed them twice a day, not too much either time. That way they stay healthy and alert. If no one has any questions, I'll see you in a week." And he left.

The dogs were still sitting there, looking at everybody.

"Brownie, what do you think of you and Brazos handling the dogs for a few days? We can gradually add everyone in. Maybe that way, we won't confuse them or ourselves too much." Jim suggested.

"Sounds good to me but I need to study that sheet to learn those hand signals. These dogs haven't moved since he signaled them to sit. I need to know how to make them move."

Brazos smiled, "Me, too. Those are beautiful animals and at this point, I think they're smarter than we are." Everyone laughed.

Sue was watching the dogs. "After you men learn what's to do, I'll try."

Jim laughed. "I'm going to be last on the list. You will be the ones working with them, so all of you learn first. I definitely feel better knowing that we have some four legged friends to help keep watch. These nuts haven't given up yet. They're still after Sue and me. It will be a couple more days before I feel up to getting on a horse, so I'm stuck at the house. Sue can't ride out either. They may take a shot at her."

About that time, a pickup came rolling into the yard. When it stopped, Don and Tom got out.

Jim welcomed them, "Hello, come meet our new crew." Don and Tom walked into the barn. The dogs were still sitting there.

Jim said, "Meet Andy and Barney, the new night guards. Put your hand out and let them smell you, pet and talk to them."

They did that and Tom made the hand signal used to tell the dogs lay down.

The men looked surprised and Tom laughed, "I know Black Jack and I know his dogs. He's trained some for me."

Brownie and Brazos smiled, "We could use some help with the hand signals. We're going to work with the dogs first and then let the other men work their way in until all of us know how to work them."

"No problem. Let's practice a few now while Don talks to Jim and Sue. Come on." With that, Tom signaled the dogs, they got up and followed him around to the side of the barn.

"We hope they didn't see the dogs arrive. Black Jack doesn't advertise his business. Let's go in the house. I need to sit down."

Don followed him. "You do look a little worse for wear."

Jim shook his head. "I don't recommend standing too close to a blast."

Chapter 15

JIM, SUE, MASON and Don sat at the table. Irene poured coffee and served slices of chocolate cake.

Don said, "That hit the spot. Thanks, Irene." She just waved a hand and kept preparing dinner.

Don inquired, "Sue, have you made up your mind about the second test well? This one is in and capped. The oil company will be out to set up a deal with you. You know anything about that end of the business?"

"No, I don't. Who do you think Jim and I should talk to? I'm not money hungry but I do want the best deal I can get." Sue said as she looked at Don.

"You'll need to talk to an oil lease attorney. Here's the name of a man I've dealt with before. He will give you a fair deal. Depending on how much oil they want to pump, you could see quite an increase in your income."

Jim said soberly, "We got another threat on our lives, on the email account. Whoever they are, they haven't given up yet."

Don shook his head, "I don't understand people like that. It's not their property, but they still want it."

Sue said quietly, "Go for the second well, in for a penny, in for a pound. Not that I want more wells, but do you think there is a chance there could be oil somewhere else on the property?"

Don was quiet as he thought about Sue's question. "I don't know. I haven't looked the property over. I would have to ride across it and look for sign."

Sue shrugged, "I was just thinking that maybe there's enough here to support several wells and that's why they want it so bad. Two wells would make a nice extra income but is it worth killing a man over?"

"When you put it like that, there may be more oil here but if you're not interested in it, I wouldn't go looking for it. Will you let me choose the site for the second test well or do you want to choose it?"

Sue shook her head, "You choose. I can't, in safety, ride out there. If I take a man with me, that makes him a target, too. And Jim is not up to riding yet."

Don replied, "Okay, then. I'll move the drilling platform and rig to a site I choose, and get the second test well going. I wasn't trying to rush you but the equipment is here already. If I move it out and then you decide you want it, then I have to move it all back in and it will be worse on the road we made. This way, when I leave, I won't come back and nature will soon take over."

Don rose to his feet. "Let's go, Tom. We have a second well to drill."

Tom grinned, "Good for you, Sue. Hope it hits too." Don and Tom left.

Sue went back to the kitchen.

Jim turned to Mason, "What did the dealer say when you told him his truck was blown up?"

"The first thing he asked was whether any one was killed. I told him you were hurt, but on the mend, and that it was just by chance that you weren't killed. I told him about the dirt in the fuel line. He said he never had that kind of trouble before, but was glad the first time saved lives. He can send an insurance adjuster when I get finished going through the truck. Between his insurance and your insurance, he wasn't worried. He would just pick out another one to use for his loaner. Said he would call you when yours was finished, which it almost is, and for you to not worry about calling him."

Mason nodded, "Those two men have been as good as gold. I consider them friends."

Jim and Sue nodded, Jim added, "We consider you in there with them. When this is over, we'll have a big barbeque and all of you are invited."

Mason grinned, "I'll be here. Besides, I have to keep an eye on my foal's mother."

Sue laughed, "She's not a mother yet."

"But she will be." Mason smiled.

Chapter 16

MASON'S PHONE RANG and he went outside to answer it. He was back in a minute.

"My friend said for me to get there in a hurry. He didn't want to say more on the phone. I don't know what time I'll be back. Let the men know, please."

Jim nodded, "Okay. Be careful, Mason. These men are nuts. They don't mind killing people and I don't think they would stop because you're the law, in fact you might be even more at risk."

"I'll be cautious. You two stay safe here and Irene, would you mind saving some dinner for me?"

"Like I never do," Irene laughed. Then Mason left.

Jim slowly made his way to the bunkhouse. Before he got there, one of the dogs came up to him, then turned and walked away. Jim thought I'll have to learn to tell them apart. When he got to the bunkhouse, he knocked and Brownie let him in. It was neat and clean with beds made, clothes hanging neatly, and no trash sitting out.

Jim sat down, "Mason just left. He got an urgent call from his friend to come at once, we don't know why. He didn't know when he would be back but plans to come back tonight. He wanted the guards to know to expect him. How are you doing with the dogs? One met me, smelled me and walked off."

Brownie replied, "Tom was a big help. It was easy to grasp the signals after he showed us. And they're just like the pictures."

"Are the dogs doing alright?"

"Yep, we walked them around the perimeter of the ranch yard, house, barn and trailers. They have been checking ever since. They go into the barn to one of the guards, rest a few minutes, and they are gone again. Tom said they would approach you in a different way when they sense a problem. They know everyone in this area and they won't get too close to someone they don't know, so we learn as we go. Like I said before, the dogs are smarter than we are." Everyone laughed.

"Okay." Jim stood up and slowly made his way to the cook house.

"How are you doing, Cookie?" he asked.

Cookie grinned, "Better than you. I just went into a ditch, but you had to blow up a truck."

Jim laughed, "That I did, and it wasn't my truck. That was the loaner. I don't recommend blowing up a truck." Jim shook his head.

Cookie laughed, "It's a write off for the dealer. You made his day."

"Need anything from town?"

Cookie quickly answered. "No, and if I did, you are not going to go pick it up. You just sit your butt at home until you look like you could fight your way out of a paper sack."

Jim grinned, "Okay. I'm going into the house now." He smiled all the way back, even when one of the dogs checked on him again. He made it in the house, told Sue and Irene he was tired and was going upstairs to bed.

Sue advised, "Take a dose of your medicine first, Jim."

Jim smiled, "Yes, ma'am, I'll do that. I want to get to feeling better, so I'll follow Doctor Sue's orders." Sue and Irene's smiles broke into contagious laughter. Jim felt like he'd been run over by a truck. He made his way slowly up the stairs, showered, took his medicine and was asleep in just a few minutes. Sue checked on him before going to her room, she was worried and hoped he would feel better in the morning.

Sue woke up earlier than Jim did now that he was hurt. Mason hadn't made it back to the house last night. The men were getting anxious to start cutting fire wood, all the delays meant that they might not have enough for winter. They knew that they couldn't leave the ranch and house unprotected. While Brownie and Sue were discussing it, Jim came downstairs. He was moving a lot better than the day before. Sue told Jim what they were discussing. Jim wanted to know how far away they cut it, and whether it was accessible by horseback.

Sue and Brownie thought about it, Brownie answered, "We don't usually ride horses there, but we do use the sled to bring the wood home. "We usually just take one horse out to pull it back, but I guess we could ride horses and be able to get back to the house pretty quick."

"Do this. Ride your horses, leave two men here on guard duty. With the dogs moving around, that should be plenty. Have one man on guard while you cut the wood, swapping out so that one man doesn't only have to do guard duty. If we have trouble, and shots are fired, leave the sled and come back here. It may mean a little extra time to get the necessary wood, but it beats running out of wood and heat. Is that okay with you, Sue?"

"If the men can work it out, it's fine with me. Brownie, do you think the men will go for it?"

Brownie replied, "Yes. The two guards in the barn can swap out and get in some time wood cutting the next day, and so on until everybody has had a turn. We will need a lot of wood this year. We have a bigger cook shack and Cookie's bedroom to keep warm, so we need to get started on that pretty soon."

Jim nodded, "Okay. Set it up and let us know when you leave. If you have trouble while cutting wood, fire your gun three times and we'll come help you. Have your guard stand off a ways so he can hear any shots from here."

"We'll get things ready to go right away," Brownie replied and he left.

Sue told Jim that Mason didn't make it back last night.

"Sure hope everything is okay. He's a good man but

he's only one man." Jim said he needed something to do. He didn't feel like riding yet but he was getting bored. Sue and Irene laughed at him.

"Men make the worst patients."

Jim shrugged and grinned, "Think I'll get that sheet with the hand signals on it and study them. Sue, maybe you could make enough copies everyone could have one."

"I can do that and I'll laminate each so they won't tear or wear out. They will most likely get a lot of handling."

"I'll go get the master copy." He went to the bunk house just as men were getting ready to leave to cut wood.

He went into the barn where the dogs were resting. Brazos was on guard, sitting where Jim couldn't see him.

"Need anything?"

"No, just looking around and checking things out. I'm kind of tired of being housebound." The men both laughed.

Jim went back into the house. Sue made a copy for each of the hands and laminated them. Jim took them down to the bunk house, and gave one to Cookie who looked at it and shook his head.

"You can do a lot of weird things now." Jim laughed and went back to the house.

"Sue, have you called that oil lease lawyer yet?"

"Not yet. Let me get the number and you get on the other phone and see if we can set up an appointment with him out here."

"I won't say anything unless he steps out of line."

"I'm dialing the number. Okay, pick it up now. His name is Alex Reynolds." The phone was answered by his secretary, but she put the call right through.

"Mr. Reynolds, your name was given to me by Don Thomas. He just brought in a well for me. I would like to talk to you about what I can expect and what I can get. He said you would do a fair deal. Are you interested?"

Mr. Reynolds replied, "Yes, I'm interested. Don Thomas is an honest and trustworthy man. When can we meet?"

"There is a problem with that. There have been several attempts made on my life recently. Someone is trying to take my ranch away from me. I don't feel safe leaving, can you come out to the ranch?"

Mr. Reynolds replied, "Under those circumstances, I will certainly make the trip. Tell me where you are and how to get there. When would you like to schedule a meeting?"

"When is a good time for you? I'll be home for the foreseeable future."

Mr. Reynolds, "I can be there tomorrow about one, is that okay with you?"

Sue replied, "Try to make it a little earlier and we'll have lunch. I have a house keeper who's a very good cook. You don't want to miss out on that."

Mr. Reynolds laughed, "Okay, make it about noon.

See you tomorrow." Jim and Sue hung up.

"You okay with that, Jim?"

"Yes, and I think we can take Don's word for him. Wonder if Irene has something to eat." Sue laughed and shook her head.

Chapter 17

MASON GOT IN about three that afternoon. He looked beat.

"Things are moving pretty fast now. I can't tell you what we are doing, so you'll have to take my word for it. My friend got some info from our last guests and we're moving on it. I'm sorry I can't tell you more but I can't. Will you trust me?" Jim and Sue nodded yes.

"Okay. I need to eat something, get a shower, catch a nap then I've got to go back. Like I said, things are moving fast."

"Irene just fed us a great dinner a couple hours ago, so she has something for you to eat whenever you are ready."

"Thanks, I'm starving. I just might chase one of those dogs down and see if I can eat him."

Irene, "Oh, you won't have to go so far as that. Here, sit down and eat." She placed a plate piled high with smoked brisket, roasted potatoes, and his favorite salad on the table in front of him. When he finished that, she gave him a slice of hot apple pie with a slice of cheese on it.

"I think I might survive now. I was beginning to get a little weak in the knees. I'm off to bed if you could wake me up at about eight." and left.

Jim studied the hand signal sheet. Sue went into the

office. She was caught up on her paper work so she decided to work on the plans for a garden and flower beds. She got interested in them and before she knew it, Irene called them in to eat. Sue told Irene about the guest they were expecting for lunch the next day and asked her to make something special.

After they ate, Jim went out to talk to the men, "How did it go cutting firewood today? Did you get a lot accomplished?"

Brownie answered for the men. "It went pretty well, but we also need to check on the herd. We've been ignoring them for a few days while all this other stuff has been going on. I'll ride over and check on them tomorrow while they're cutting wood."

"Okay. But keep the guard away from the saws so he can hear shots if you have any trouble."

Brownie nodded. "Okay. That will work."

Jim shook his head, "I'll sure be glad when I feel like riding again. As sore as I am, there isn't much I can do. I didn't know getting blown up could hurt in so many places."

Brownie was very serious. "Jim, you're alive. That's what is important." All the men agreed.

Jim nodded and answered, "Mason got in about three this afternoon. Said things were getting real busy but he couldn't tell us anything. He said to trust him, so we will. He got something to eat and went to bed. He was beat when he came in. I'm going to wake him about eight tonight and he'll be leaving again. We also have an appointment tomorrow with an oil lease lawyer about noon. Sue promised the lawyer a good meal if he would make the trip here as she can't leave the house. We'll spring me on him tomorrow. Don Thomas said he would make us a fair deal on the oil lease, so that's what we're going for. His name is Alex Reynolds, so let the guards know. You men find your hand signal sheets okay?"

"Yep, those are nice."

"Sue did them for you." Jim told them.

"Tell her "Thank you".

"I will do that. I'm about ready to hit the bed, too. See you tomorrow. Good night."

"Good night, Jim." Jim went into the house.

"Sue, I'm about ready to go to bed. Would you wake Mason around eight, please?"

"I can sure do that Jim. Be sure to take your medicine before you go to bed."

"I will. I still don't have my strength back. I feel like it's taking too long."

"No, it isn't. You were nearly hit with that blast and being knocked down and having a concussion, took a lot out of you. Just don't rush things, you're improving each day. You stay up a little more each day. You walk a little more each day. Jim, you were almost killed in that blast, so be patient, please."

"Okay. I'll grin and try to be patient."

Sue chuckled. "That's the way! Now, take your medicine and go to bed."

Jim said with a little salute, "Yes, ma'am." Jim climbed the stairs, took a shower, took his medicine, got into bed and was a sleep in just a few minutes.

At eight o'clock, Sue knocked on Mason's door.

"Yes?"

"Mason, it's eight o'clock. It's time for you to wake up. Irene has some food ready for you. I'll see you down stairs."

Mason dressed and grabbed his computer case and was down stairs in a few minutes. He looked around for Jim.

"Jim went to bed early. He still hasn't recovered from that blast and concussion."

"I think we almost lost him that day. Had he been just one step closer, he may not have survived."

"That's what I told him when he was complaining about how slowly he's recovering."

Mason said, "A lot depends on what I find when I get back to my friend. I'll be in touch with you later."

Mason ate the plate of food Irene placed in front of him. When he finished, he pushed his plate aside.

He complimented Irene. "That was very good. Thank you." She just waved his thanks aside.

Mason inquired, "Anything I need to know here on

the home front?"

"I have an oil lease lawyer coming tomorrow. Don Thomas recommends him."

"He should be okay, then. Well, I better get going. Most likely I won't return tonight. Wish us luck tonight."

"My prayers are with you. Be safe and be careful." Mason touched his hat in a salute, grabbed his computer case and left.

Sue told Irene she was going into the office. She got her plans out for the garden and flower beds, then turned and walked back to the kitchen.

"Irene, what kind of herbs would you plant in a garden?"

Irene looked at her, "There are several kinds you can plant, depending on the kind of seasoning you want and like. Also, you can plant herbs in pots and raise them year round on the window sill. Why?"

"Jim told me to plan a garden and flower beds as something for me to do. You may not know it, but I was a hired hand here after you left. Whatever the men did, I did. I also cooked for everyone, cleaned the house, did the laundry for Hawk and myself, and did most of the paper work in the office. I kept the recordings of births, brandings, and expenses. That's why I have such a hard time sitting still."

Irene looked surprised, "You did all that? Oh honey, I'm sorry."

"Yes, Hawk taught me everything. He insisted that I

learn all aspects of the ranch so that when he was gone, I could run it and know if someone was trying to cheat me. I didn't know anyone was trying to take the ranch. It broke my heart when he gave it to Jim. I understand now, he was trying to save it for me. He knew Jim would give it back to me when things were okay. Jim has promised to do just that, and he will."

Irene said, "Bring your plans in here and we'll take a look at them." They spent the next hour going over plans for the garden, what to plant, when to plant, and herbs for the garden.

"Irene, are you happy here?"

"Yes I am. I enjoy my job and being out here. A lot has changed since last time I was here with you, but it still feels like home."

Sue replied, "I don't know what Jim and I would do without you. Will you stay on? For as long as you want to?"

Irene looked at Sue, "You're in love with him, aren't you?"

Sue was quiet for a few minute. She had lost her mother when she was very young. Hawk had made sure she was well-cared for, in fact, he did most of it himself. So she had not had another woman to take into her confidence, except for Grace, for a long time. It wasn't easy for her to share her feelings, but with Irene's warm-hearted love, she found herself carrying on about Jim in no time.

"I think I'm falling in love with him. I know my life wouldn't be complete without him. He told me this place was beginning to feel like home to him. If he'll stay, I will give him half of the ranch. It's only fair after what he's done, and we could continue operating it as one ranch. We've kissed a few times and he seems interested. I'll wait for him. I almost lost him when that truck blew up and I don't want to experience that again."

Irene listened thoughtfully before replying. "If you and Jim want me to stay, I will. I love it here. I enjoy cooking for you, and the house work isn't bad at all. So you and Jim talk it over and let me know. If you'll let me help, we'll have one OUTSTANDING garden next year. The flower beds will be up to you. The next time I'm in town, I'll see what I can pick up to raise in pots through the winter."

"That's great, Irene. I guess I am off to bed, good night." Sue quietly checked on Jim before going into her own room.

The next morning, Jim was up early.

When he walked into the kitchen for coffee, Irene asked, "Are you feeling better today? At least, you look better and you're moving better."

Jim laughed, "See what happens when you follow the doctor's orders? Hope I don't need any more of that medicine, though. The roof could fall in and I would never know it. I'll check with the men and be back in for breakfast."

"Brownie, how did the herd look yesterday?"

"They're just fine. They still have a lot of good grass so they aren't tempted to wander off. We got more wood cut, and plan to start bringing it in tomorrow. We still have a lot to cut. We're not complaining, just making a statement. It's our butts that will be cold if we don't have enough firewood ready come winter time."

"Is everyone pitching in and doing their fair share?"

"Oh, yeah, each of us makes sure the other one does his share. It's a joint effort. The sled is almost full so we'll take a horse to pull it back. Then, we all get a chance at stacking it. We split it pretty even between the cook house and the bunk house. It's easier in the long run. We have to get wood for the main house, too. By the way, you're looking better this morning, moving better, too."

"Yeah, I'm getting there. It's slow. Hope I don't need any more of that medicine. Like I told Irene, the roof could fall in and I would sleep through it."

The men laughed, "Enjoy it while you can. I look for all hell to break lose again. Just don't know when, it's been too quiet. I think they're planning something."

"Is everybody learning to handle the dogs?"

"Yeah, after Tom showed me and Brazos, we showed everyone else, and they picked it up pretty fast. They are good dogs. Black Jack knows what he's doing. We've been able to sleep a little better at night, knowing that they're out there keeping watch"

"You think they would be a good investment, then?"
"Yes, I do."
"Okay. Go ahead and get started on the day, be careful and be safe." Jim went into the house. Sue was up by this time and Irene had breakfast on the table.

Chapter 18

AFTER THEY HAD eaten, Sue asked Jim to go into the office with her. She sat down behind the desk and he sat in one of the arm chairs.

"Jim, do you like Irene?"

Jim was surprised by the question, but answered, "Yes, I do like Irene. I think of her sometimes as my second mom."

"I asked her last night to stay on and make her home here with us. She said she would like to if we agreed. Jim, are you beginning to think of The Six Killer Ranch as your home?"

Jim replied, "Yes, Sue. It's becoming home to me. Do you want me to stay?"

"Yes. If you stay, I'll make you half owner of the ranch."

"Sue, I don't need part of the ranch. I told you, the ranch belongs to you."

"But if you stay, you deserve part of it. You almost lost your life protecting me and the ranch. Hawk chose the right man when he chose you."

"Sue, I think I'm falling for you. It's been a long time since I cared for some one. I move very slowly. I think you care a little for me, let's see where it goes. Hopefully, this mess will soon be over and we can get on with our lives.

Will you agree to that?"

Although she'd been sure that Jim felt the same way as she did before mentioning it, Sue felt like a huge weight had been lifted, and her heart filled with joy.

Sue smiled, "If you agree to half ownership in the ranch. When this is settled, we'll have the papers drawn up. I know the men respect and like you. I've never seen the three old hands take to a man like they have to you. We'll have the finest crew you can find anywhere. Now, let's make a list of questions we want to ask our guest after lunch."

Their guest arrived about noon. He introduced himself, showed picture ID and produced a copy of his license. Jim and Sue introduced themselves, then led him into the kitchen, introduced him to Irene. She had lunch on the table. They all sat down and ate.

When they were finished, he said, "Sue, Irene's cooking lived up to everything you told me. It was worth coming a little early to enjoy such a meal. Now, if you will, please explain things to me."

Jim and Sue took turns telling him everything that had happened.

Alex said thoughtfully, "As things stand now, Jim owns the ranch, correct?"

"Yes."

Alex nodded, "Okay. We need to put the lease in both your names. The income will be split in half."

"But I'm giving Sue the ranch back as soon as this mess is cleared up."

Alex explained, "That's okay, but NOW, the oil well will have to belong to both of you, what you decide to do with the property at a later time, has no effect on the oil lease. With someone trying so hard to get this property, we want to write into the oil lease that any other wells that are drilled and come in still belong to the both of you."

"Don is drilling a second test well now in the same area." Sue explained.

Alex nodded. "We will include that one in the lease, with all the same stipulations. Knowing Don, it will be coming in just like the first one."

"That's all we want to drill, just these two wells. But I think there must be more oil on the property. Two wells will make a nice income but not enough to kill a man over and that's what we believe happened to my dad. With all the attempts made on us, it just figures there is more to it. Jim isn't over that blast and concussion yet. Had we both still been in the truck, we both would have died that day."

Alex shook his head, "Some people are so greedy. I hope the law catches them."

"We don't figure we can get them for Hawk's death, but attempted murder is a sure thing," Jim said.

Alex nodded. "Okay. Now, as for your pay, this is the standard pay for oil per gallon pumped from your wells.

This is what I offer everyone. No special deals. When the wells start pumping, it will surprise you how much money you can make. With two wells, you'll see a difference real quick. Do you have any questions? I'll have my secretary type up the leases and I'll bring them back for your signatures, so Irene can feed me again."

Irene laughed, "That sounds fine."

Alex was serious now. "There are no decals on my doors, and I don't know anyone around here, so nobody should know what we have discussed. You two take care and stay safe."

Jim and Sue replied in unison, "Drive safe."

"Sue, are you satisfied with the deal?"

"Yes, are you?" Sue asked.

Jim shook his head. "I really didn't want my name on the lease. I promised to give everything back to you, now I can't."

Sue was smiling, "That's okay. I think of it as half yours anyway." Irene grinned, thinking that things just might work out between the two of them, despite all the tragedy they had been through.

"Jim. Let's go check on the mare. We haven't had a chance to check her out. I need something to keep busy. Irene has already cleaned up the kitchen, washed the laundry and dusted the living room. That doesn't leave much for me to do. I can't plant a garden or flower bed, too late in the year. By the way, Irene, Jim wants you to stay, too."

With that, Jim walked over and hugged her, "Please stay, Mom Number Two." Irene had tears in her eyes while she shoved him out the door.

Jim and Sue walked to the barn. Sue went first to pet Red, give him a sugar cube, and brush him down. The whole time he was trying to bump her with his head. Jim stood outside the stall and watched, laughing at them as they played. It was an awesome sight, seeing that huge stallion acting so gentle with Sue. He loved her and it showed. When she finished with him, she forked hay into his stall, turned on the water, and shut the gate, while Red watched intently.

Jim led the mare out of her stall. She was a well-built horse with coloring would go well with Red's. They walked her around a little while to see how she moved, brushed her down, checked her teeth and hooves. She kept butting Sue, wanting a sugar cube. She was mild-mannered and didn't get upset when one of the dogs came near her.

"I think we made a good choice," Sue said happily.

"So do I. She's long legged, moves easily and doesn't seem to shy. She likes to be handled. Let's put her back in her stall. I'd like to ride her sometime, after this mess is over."

Sue nodded, "Me, too. I can't wait to get out and about.

"Hopefully soon, but for now I suppose we need to get back to the house."

On the way back, Jim reminded Sue, "Don't forget the guards in the barn. They could see and hear us talking. We have a pretty good idea of where we're going so give it time. I need to fill you in on my life before we met, but not right now. We need time alone for that."

"I would love to know all about your life Jim, I look forward to it."

Before they entered the house, Mason drove up. He got out, looking as exhausted as if he had been gone for days.

"I have a lot to tell you but I need a shower to wake up enough to eat first. While I'm getting cleaned up could you ask Irene to fix me a big plate, I'm starved. I'll meet you two at the table in a few minutes." He went upstairs and they went into the kitchen. Jim told Irene what Mason said and she got busy, putting the finishing touches to dinner.

"May as well sit down, I'll feed all of you now. Dinner will be ready by the time Mason gets back down here anyway." Mason was down about twenty minutes later. They let him enjoy a relaxing meal before pressuring him for details.

"It's almost over. Just as I guessed, one of the men talked to save his hide. When the others found out, they were all talking, trying to outdo one another, hoping for leniency from the judge. We managed to get all of the information we need, including names and phone numbers.

They were naming people we didn't know were involved. That's why it's taken so long to get to the bottom of it. There was a large oil cartel involved. People you don't know and have probably never heard of."

Mason looked down for a moment before looking Sue in the eye. He knew his next words were going to hurt her.

"I'm sorry to have to tell you Sue, but Ryder was one of the men that put the plan together. No wonder he tried to talk Hawk out of naming Jim King as his heir. One of the men knew about Jim. By the way, Jim, I'm glad you were on our side. You have quite a rep for bringing down these types of people. Your problem here was that it was all underground."

Jim glanced toward Sue, knowing that he hadn't had an opportunity to share his past yet.

Mason continued, "The oil cartel knew the only way to deal with you was to take you out entirely. They sure tried hard enough. Ryder thought you would come to him for help and he could steer the men right to you."

"Sue, Ryder seemed to figure you didn't know anything about ranching. Then after Hawk was gone, they realized he had taught you how to run the ranch, so they felt like they had to take you out, too. We found the two wounded men. The one we thought got nicked a little, ended up with a bullet hole in his arm. And Irene, your man was full of infection. They hadn't taken him to a Doctor or hospital because they knew we had placed alerts out for anyone who came in with a buckshot butt. Irene, you really gave him a problem. He'll be lying on his stomach for a long time. If we had not found him when we did, he most likely would have died from blood poisoning, so that's another charge against them."

"We had a man on Ryder but he seems to be out of town. You won't see the whole story in the papers. We'll keep most of it for the court appearance. But as far as I know, it's over. You can get back to your lives or start a new one."

Jim asked, "What about the dealer's truck?"

"His insurance adjuster will be there tomorrow. When you pick up your own truck, you can show him your insurance papers and let the adjuster advise both of you."

Sue turned to Mason, "When do you leave again?"

"I'll have to leave today when I finish up here. But I'll be back tomorrow to say goodbye. I need to tie up some loose ends tonight."

"Can you take a few minutes and tell the men? They've been through hell and stood by us through everything. Just give them a quick rundown, I'll go out and see if I can answer any questions."

Mason agreed, "I can do that. That's the least they deserve."

Jim and Sue walked him to the door just as Don drove up. He was grinning ear to ear. "It's in, Sue, your second well blew about an hour ago."

Mason said, "That's great! Don, come into the bunk house with me. Brownie, get all the men together, I have a story to tell." About fifteen minutes later, they heard Mason drive down the road.

Don came into the house, "Well, it seems like things have worked out for you. Glad it's over? "

Jim and Sue both said, "Oh yes, it's taken over our lives."

Don was smiling. "I'm glad I brought the news about the well, it just capped things off, you might say. I'll see you both before I leave."

"How long will it take to dismantle everything and get it ready to move?" Sue asked.

"It will take three to four days to tear it down and load it. We'll use the last of the water in the tanker to settle the dust as we leave," Don replied.

"Be sure you and ALL the men come by on your way out." Sue told him.

Don replied, "We will," and left.

Jim went to the bunkhouse, "Did Don say anything to you men?"

"No."

"The other well came in a little over an hour ago. So now there are two oil wells on the property." The men were happy for Jim and Sue, but were happier about the news Mason brought.

"Mason explained it a little better to us but we wanted

him to tell you, it's now a closed chapter out here. The lawyer that Hawk trusted all these years, sold him out. That's why he tried to talk him out of giving me the ranch. He felt like they had a better chance of taking over with Sue in charge. He wasn't prepared for her ability and knowledge about the ranch and its operation. Do you have any questions?"

Irene's eyes were blazing, livid with anger. Sue had never seen her so upset. "Never could trust that lawyer Ryder," she said, "I couldn't afford a divorce lawyer and he represented that no-good I was married to. I had a little piece of tribal land from my grandmother, and I know it is not legal but he is living out there with his girlfriend, and Ryder helped him do it. It's nothing compared to what he has done to you, but he had better watch over his shoulder. I wonder how many more people he's hurt and taken advantage of."

"Why were they so set on killing you, Jim?"

"Some of the oil cartel knew about me. I can tell you more but I owe it to Sue to tell her first."

Brownie nodded, "Be sure to fill us in, Jim."

"I have no problem telling you, but not until she knows the whole story. Her dad trusted me to save the ranch for her, and with a lot of help from all of you, I think that was accomplished. Are you men going to cut wood tomorrow?"

Brownie shook his head. "No. I think we'll take the

day off and do some odd jobs that we've let go recently."

Jim agreed. "We will talk tomorrow then." He went inside the house.

Sue and Irene were sitting at the table with three cups of coffee.

Sue simply said, "Time for you to talk, Jim."

"I know." He sat silent for a short time. "A little more than ten years ago, my wife and I had a small ranch. It was all we wanted, just enough for one man to manage. She raised a garden, and planted flower beds everywhere she could dig new ground. She kept flowers in the house all spring, summer and late into the fall. We started having some problems on the ranch. I found out who was causing it and how. The men got mad when I caught them. One night, they fired into the house. They hit my wife and killed her. After that, I pursued them and brought them to court. They were found guilty and they are still serving time."

Jim continued without looking at either woman, lost in his memory, "I met Hawk about then. I wasn't happy living out on the ranch without my wife, life wasn't the same. The killers had ruined it for me and I was at loose ends. Hawk gave me a name and told me to go visit him, to tell him my story and see what developed. I sold everything after I met him, and became a range detective. I knew my way around a ranch, knew what to look for. I took to the job like a duck to water."

Jim looked at Sue, taking in her beauty, "Hawk kept tabs on me by letters, writing every once in a while, to my headquarters. He knew that was the only sure place that he could eventually reach me. That's how he got in touch with me when he realized he needed my help. He was depending on me to help him solve his problems. I had made a name for myself in clearing ranch problems. I was actually already on my way here when headquarters called and told me that Hawk was dead. I didn't know what to do so I turned and went back. That's where Ryder got in touch with me and told me I had to be here for the reading of the will."

With a beseeching look, hoping she would believe him, Jim said, "Sue, Ryder did NOT tell me that Hawk had given me the ranch. It was as much of a shock to me as it was to you. I only knew I had to save the ranch for you because Hawk knew I wouldn't keep it. I haven't owned a place or put down roots since I sold my own place. Sue, my reputation is what nearly got you killed several times. Are you sure you want me to stay now that you know the whole story? We'll have to find another lawyer to get the papers drawn up so I can turn the ranch over to you."

Sue replied quickly, "I want you to stay on and the papers will show part ownership for both of us. We are partners, in the ranch and in the oil wells. We'll see what else we're partners in."

Jim asked them both, "Do you have any more questions?"

Sue shook her head, "Not about you. How about a barbecue before Don, Tom and their men, and Mason have to leave? I also want to give our men a bonus, a little more for the older hands as they had the most responsibilities. They deserve extra pay for the way they defended this ranch and us, besides doing all the work. Are we going to keep the dogs? Do we need those dogs now? Or just run of the mill puppies?"

Jim laughed, "Whoa! That's a whole bunch of questions, woman. The barbecue, that sounds good. Bonus for the men, that's good, too. I have no problem with that. How about a Christmas bonus? As for the dogs, they are well-trained, but maybe more than what we need here on the ranch now. Maybe Black Jack has a couple of puppies he wants to sell. He could still sell these dogs and we'll give him what he thinks we owe for the week we had them. A little training wouldn't hurt the puppies so they would stay out from under the horse's hooves, and not startle them. We can call him, tell him what we have in mind and ask him to the barbecue. Let's take care of it tomorrow after Mason gets back and we're sure all the bad men are in jail. It's been too sudden and I still can't believe it's over."

Chapter 19

"WHEN IS ALEX supposed to be back? Maybe he can be our lawyer. I sure don't trust anyone around here," Jim asked.

Sue suggested, "Why don't you call Alex and tell him to be here for the barbecue. We will kill two birds with one stone that way."

Jim shook his head and said, "Sue, that's not the best saying to quote right now."

Sue smiled and put her hand over her mouth, "Oops."

"I'm tired. I'm going to head off to bed."

"Take your medicine," Sue reminded him.

"No, I'm not taking any more. The roof could fall in and I would not know it till I tried to get up in the morning." Sue and Irene laughed at Jim.

"Well, Irene what do you think?" Sue asked after Jim went upstairs.

"I think you're right. He is still a little leery about owning half the ranch and that speaks highly for him. Give him time, he'll come around. He's still a little touchy, but only a little, about his wife dying. He knows he didn't do it. The men shooting into his house are the guilty ones, and he made sure they were punished." Irene said as she reflected on what Jim had told them.

"I feel the same way. What could we, you and I, do as something special for the men to say 'thank you'?" Sue asked.

"I don't know. Let me think on it for a while. The bunk house and cook house are both set up pretty well and Cookie is a good cook. I'll check with him and see how he varies the food. Maybe he'll have an idea," Irene replied.

"I'm going to bed. Maybe I can take Red for a ride tomorrow. It's been so long and I miss riding him," Sue commented as she left to retire.

The next morning everyone was up early. Brownie went to check on the herd. They would need to move them back to the lower pasture for the winter.

Grace backed her car from the garage carefully and headed out to the ranch. She wanted to talk to Sue and Jim about the latest happenings but couldn't leave the boarding house for any long period of time. So this morning she headed out immediately after breakfast was finished.

She felt that it was strange when Ryder came by to offer his sympathy about Joe's demise as he called it. Demise hell, Grace thought, more like murder, pure and simple, and she thought Ryder was responsible. She thought he must have been poking around for clues, checking to see if she was suspicious or whether Joe had told her anything before he left.

Then there was the stranger. He had come in and

stayed for a few days, then just disappeared one day, along with some of the things from the office down stairs. She was usually very selective about who she let stay, but money was tight these days, so against her better judgment she'd taken him in.

Grace had always felt that Ryder was only interested in money, and she knew Joe's estate would not amount to anything. She barely knew the lawyer so his stopping by seemed odd at the time, and stranger now that her suspicions had been raised. She mused about all the possibilities while driving to see Jim and Sue.

Jim and Sue were just heading out the door to check cattle, and Brownie and Cookie were preparing to go to town for supplies as Grace pulled into the yard.

She could sense their concern as they headed into the office. Grace told them how she felt and after hearing that Mason had solved the case, she wondered if they could pin Joe's death on Ryder as well. Mason assured her that he would look into it.

When Grace left for town, she was feeling more righteous indignation than Sue thought possible given her gentle accepting nature. She commented that Joe may have been a very unsophisticated person, but he was a good man, decent, and honorable, which was more than could be said of most people, and she was not through seeking justice.

Sue, Jim, and Irene all agreed but felt rather powerless

to help her in her quest.

Jim called Black Jack and explained the basics situation to him. Black Jack said he had some puppies that would work better as pets. Jim asked him to the barbeque and said they could switch and settle up then.

Next, he called Alex and asked if he could be their personal lawyer along with being their oil lease lawyer. Alex said he didn't see why it wouldn't work.

"Why not use Hawk's long time lawyer?" he asked.

Jim replied, "He's not available and won't be for a long time. He'll be spending his time in jail."

Alex said, "Oh. That's too bad. It is a bad reflection on our profession."

Jim agreed. "Yes, it is. We're going to have a barbecue to celebrate the end of this, would you like to join us?"

Alex quickly answered, "Yes, I would. When should I arrive?"

"I'll let you know. We're trying to set up a time that works for everyone, so I will get back to you. By the way, the second oil well came in yesterday, so you'll need paper work to cover that one, too. When you come, plan on staying a while, Sue and I have some things that we need to have taken care of."

Alex agreed, "Okay. Let me know the date and time."

"I will."

Jim asked Sue if she had anyone else she wanted to invite. Sue said no but maybe the men had a girlfriend they wanted to invite.

"I'll ask them. When Brownie gets back I need to talk to them. They want to know why I was targeted. I told them I would explain after I talked to you."

"Okay. When can we go for a ride? I miss Red, and I want to show you our ranch."

Jim was reluctant to leave the house yet. "Let's wait for Mason and then we'll decide about the ride."

Brownie and Cookie were already on their way to town for supplies. Brownie had taken his rifle along, still feeling uncomfortable with all that had happened.

Since it was a beautiful day, Sue finally was able to convince Jim to go for a ride. There were still parts of the ranch he had never seen, and after the fresh rainfall the grass and trees were glistening with the arrival of the morning sun.

When they got back, Irene was pulling into the yard and told them she had gone to town to try to comfort Grace.

They had just finished eating when Brownie came in the door and asked to talk to Jim. Weary after the long ride, Jim asked if it could wait, but Brownie said, "No, we need to talk about this now."

He and Jim went into the office where Brownie blurted out that he and Cookie had found Ryder's body on their way home from town. Shocked, Jim asked, "What? Where? Irene just got back and she didn't say anything about seeing him?"

Brownie replied, "Well, he wasn't laying in the middle of the road. We saw some buzzards circling a ways off the main road and went to investigate. We thought maybe an old cow had died, but there he was instead. His truck was behind a little hill, out of sight of the main road. It had a flat tire, so who knows what happened. We thought we had better let you know before we told the law. Can't say we were grief stricken considering all the trouble he has caused. With Cookie being shot at, he was hardly sorry to see him either."

"After what he did to Hawk, he didn't deserve to be alive". This outburst was typical of the devotion Brownie felt to his employers and the ranch, which had been his home for most of his life.

Jim thoughtfully replied, "Well, I will have to notify Mason and the sheriff but I sure can't say I am sorry to hear it."

When he told Sue, she replied, "I thought Ryder was in custody already, but now I remember that Mason had told us he was out of town."

They had to wait for the FBI to arrive before they could go out to the site. The sheriff had blocked off the road to keep people out in the meantime. The next morning they found a gun by his body as well as a single bullet. A grand jury would be held, but with the common bullet caliber it would be difficult to ascertain whether it was a suicide or a murder. Just as with Hawk's death, the overnight rain had erased any footprints or other signs that may have led to a killer or killers.

Mason smiled to himself. There were six people he knew of with both motive and opportunity right at hand. Sue and Jim, Grace, Irene, Brownie, and Cookie all came to mind. Six possible killers connected with the Six Killer Ranch, how ironic, he thought.

Jim went to talk to the men. He told them his story, how he met Hawk and how Hawk had asked for his help, filling them in on the details of his life. He told them about the barbecue and asked if they had a girlfriend they wanted to invite, but none did. He told the men to take it easy and do any housekeeping they needed to do.

Cookie was in the cook shack when Irene slipped in. She surprised him.

Irene laughed at his expression, "I'm not after your body." He turned red.

Irene asked, "What can we, Sue and I, do special for the men to say 'Thank you'?"

"Bear sign."

Irene had a puzzled expression on her face and said, "Bear sign?"

"Yes, better known as doughnuts. I can't make them worth a damn and the men love them. I have tried a lot of times but had to throw out my errors," Cookie said.

Irene simply looked at Cookie and said, "Doughnuts".

Cookie nodded his head.

Irene said, "I'll see what I can do about some Bear sign," and went out shaking her head.

When she got back to the house, she asked Sue if she knew anything about "Bear sign".

Sue looked at her with a puzzled expression and said, "What? Bear Sign? What is that?"

Irene laughed, "Bear sign, better known as doughnuts."

Sue laughed, "There's a cookbook here somewhere that has a good doughnut recipe in it. I tried to make some and they were terrible."

"Cookie says the men love them and he can't make them worth a damn. So I guess I'll have to give it a try but not until after the barbecue. Get that recipe. We may need some things that we don't have on hand." Sue located the book and they went over the recipe several times.

Mason arrived then. He looked tired and beat up, but he was smiling, and said, "Call all the men together, that way I won't have to tell it but once."

When everyone was gathered, Mason spoke, "Okay, here goes. Everyone is picked up and in jail. NO BAIL! Attempted murder and attempted arson warrants no bail. Ryder is the one who put the deal together and offered it to the oil cartel. They slipped a man on the property and took the oil sample."

He turned towards Sue and said, "Sue, you were right, that wasn't the only oil sample taken out here. It seems like you're sitting on top of one of the biggest oil deposits in this area. There's no telling how many wells you could have if you were interested in doing that. That's the reason they wanted the ranch, not for one or two wells. I don't know all the spots they took samples from, I didn't ask as you aren't interested in drilling more wells."

Looking at Jim, Mason continued, "Jim, you were the joker in the deck. They knew your reputation and knew they had to take you out. You would easily figure out why they wanted the ranch. You're very good at your job."

"All of you men should be commended. You were an extra bonus for Jim. The cartel had no idea that you would fight to protect the ranch and the house. They thought they could come in here and ride over everybody. They found out differently, and, Irene, they respect a woman with a shot gun. If they ever get out of jail, they'll remember that, especially one. I don't know how many pieces of buck shot the hospital removed, but they said the Doctor was tired of removing them. The nurse said they lost count after about fifty."

When Mason paused, Jim asked, "So what are your plans, are you through now? Will you head back to Denver?"

"Yes, everything is finally closed down. Now, we just have to wait for the trial."

"Can you spend a day or two with us before you head back to Denver?"

"Well, I hadn't thought that far ahead. I can take a couple of days off, I guess." Mason answered thoughtfully.

Jim smiled, "We're having a barbecue and we want you here. We told Don and Tom and their men to be sure and stop here before they leave. Black Jack is coming to pick up his dogs and bring two puppies. Alex Reynolds is going to be here. He is going to be our personal lawyer along with the oil lease lawyer. All I need to do is tell everyone when to be here. Do you have a lady friend you would like to invite? She's welcome."

Mason grinned. "That sounds good to me. I'm single, no girlfriend. I'm on the lookout for one, if you know of a very nice lady." Everyone laughed.

Jim laughed the loudest. "I'll let everyone know. Now, Sue, let's take that ride to see Don and Tom and we can tell them when to be here. Oh, I need to call the butcher and see if he has a half steer for the barbecue. Does that work with everyone?"

"You bet", the men replied, with a mix of relief and happiness no one had heard in a long time. Jim made his call and Cookie was sent in to town to pick it up. The men started cleaning up an already clean yard but Jim didn't say anything.

Jim and Sue rode out to the well site. Both were capped and pumping. The men were better than half way through the take down and loading of the rig and platform.

Jim said, "We're having a barbecue day after tomorrow and you're all invited."

Don and Tom looked at Jim, "All of us?"

Jim nodded, "Every single man. We are cooking half a steer and we don't want leftovers."

Don grinned and said, "We will sure make a good start on it, this crew will."

Jim said seriously, "Come any time, and remember, when you leave, you have friends here. Stop and visit with us."

Don and Tom replied, "Thank you Jim, we will."

They mounted back up and rode out of sight before Jim stopped his horse. Sue pulled up alongside him. Jim leaned in and gave her a gentle kiss.

"Do you think you could get used to those?"

Sue smiled and replied "I think so" before passionately returning his kiss.

"Think you could get used to those?"

Jim nodded, "I am sure I can. Sue, will you marry me?"

"I would love to."

"Shall we announce our engagement at the barbecue, Sue?"

She nodded, "That would be perfect timing."

Jim told her, "We need to go to town and get you a ring."

Sue replied, "I don't need a ring Jim, I just need you."

They rode back to the ranch slowly holding hands and dreaming of their shared future.

THE END!

CPSIA information can be obtained
at www.ICGtesting.com
Printed in the USA
BVHW071050140420
577473BV00002B/186